BRUISED 2

• •

The Ultimate Revenge

A novel by Azárel

A Life Changing Book *in conjunction with* Power Play Media
Published by Life Changing Books
P. O. Box 423 Brandywine, MD 20613

This novel is a work of fiction. Any references to real people, events, establishments, or locales are intended only to give the fiction a sense of reality and authenticity. Other names, characters, and incidents occurring in the work are either the product of the author's imagination or are used fictitiously, as are those fictionalized events and incidents that involve real persons. Any character that begins to share the name of a person who is an acquaintance of the author, past or present, is purely coincidental and is in no way intended to be an actual account involving that person.

Cover design by Kevin Carr/photography by Doss Tidwell
Edited by Kathleen Jackson
Book Composition by Brian Holscher

Library of Congress Cataloging-in-Publication Data;

www.lifechangingbooks.net

ISBN *0-9741394-7-5*
Copyright ® 2006

Dedication

● ● ● ● ● ● ● ● ● ● ● ● ●

This book is dedicated to the supportive group of family members and friends who have stood by my side. You know who you are! Thank you *all* for being a blessing in my life. I could not have accomplished this task without you. Your encouragement is greatly appreciated and will never be forgotten.

introducing
Power Play
Media

in conjunction with
Life Changing Books

Acknowledgements

• • • • • • • • • • • • • • • • • • • •

Once again I've had to ask my Heavenly Father for guidance, direction, and support while completing this novel. Without You, none of this would be possible. I truly learned that I can do all things through Christ, who strengthens me. A special thanks to my husband for putting up with me!!! In 2003, I said more hot meals would be on the way. I lied. In 2005, once again, I said more hot meals would be on the way. I lied again. In 2006, I'm keeping it real. I've hired a maid! Love you for life!

Special thanks go out to all of the professionals who have worked diligently to make Bruised 2 - The Ultimate Revenge a success: Kathleen Jackson, you pulled this all together for me in the end. If it weren't for you, this document would still be on my laptop. Thanks for being there. Special thanks to Leslie Allen and Nakea Murray - without the two of you, I clearly would not be where I am today. Both of you ladies have worked on tasks above and beyond your normal duties. Whoever told me writing a book was easy, bamboozled me! Thanks for having my back.

To my parents and step-parents, I love you all dearly.

Kevin Carr of OCJGraphix.Com, the cover has heads turning. Tiffanee, our fabulous model on the cover, I can't tell you how many people are asking about your cover shot. It's hot! Shout out to Doss, the photographer. Brian Holscher, thank you so much for the book layout. Vida, thanks for coming aboard and bringing your creativity to the organization. You're exactly what we've been looking for.

Blessed is the only word that can be used to describe how I feel about the wonderful people who have been placed in my circle. I've been privileged enough to come across a fabulous group of test readers and supporters who have helped me in many aspects: Cheryl (aka "Cel"), Kim (aka "Emily"), Lisa Williams, Catina, Danielle Adams, Tonya, Danette, Tam, and Leslie G. I love each of you dearly. Believe me, I don't take your help lightly. Get ready for the next project. But don't breathe long, we've got some power hitters coming your way - fast.

A special shot out to the people who are always working the undercover publicity team; Danielle Daniels, Jeremiah, Don, Tyese, Jerri (aka. Stink), Kenya, Alaya, Janell, Wynetta, Saundra, Jackie and Jamila. Your support is greatly appreciated.

Much, much love goes out to my immediate family. There are way too many to name, but some that I must: My sister, Tam, what do I say? You are one of a kind. Let it be known, you are the accountant, babysitter, driver, board member, and your favorite - the social director. We have shared so much together, and I thank you for the support.

To my two grandmothers, Lover and Gram, and my granddaddy Toot, thanks for always having my back. I don't boast often in life, but when I speak about all of you, I can't help but to think about how blessed I am. Words can never express the gratitude, and the impact you've had and continue to have on my life.

Shout outs to all of my extended family. When I wrote the last book, some people got crazy when I forgot to mention names. Just be proud of my accomplishments and forget about my bad memory. You know I love you.

Darren Coleman (Ladies Listen Up, Do or Die, Don't Ever Wonder and Before I Let Go), thanks for being a true friend and business partner. It's amazing, you are really part of the family. Power Play Media has already been labeled a success. Keep your head up and keep doing your thing. Tyrone Wallace (Nothin' Personal and Double Life), I'm so proud of your success. People are already raving about your new book. Zach Tate (Lost and Turned Out and No Way Out), you've outdone yourself this time, the book is hot. Much love to J. Tremble (Secrets of a Housewife and More Secrets, More Lies), you worked the pen out when you wrote these red hot books. Fire!!! Tonya Ridley (The Takeover), I can't tell you what a blessing it is to have you on the team. Just know that you help me in so many ways, especially your late night jokes. Special thanks to Petey Pablo for stepping in and helping us with promotions. Danette Majette (I Shoulda Seen it Comin'), you are truly my daughter, can't wait for your next book!

Thanks to all of the distributors who have looked out for the success of Bruised 2 - The Ultimate Revenge. While I can't name them all, I'd like to especially thank the entire A&B staff (Karen, Kwame and Kevon). Thanks for looking out! Special thanks to Nati and Andy at African World Books, you are truly men of character. To all the vendors in New York and Philadelphia who hold us down at LCB, much love.

Acknowledgements

Even though my books are sold all over, I wanna especially thank the African-American bookstores. Thanks for giving our readers a place to feel at home. Emilyn at Mejah Books in Delaware, you are a phenomenal lady. Keep saving lives in your community. Keep up the good work. Karibu Books in my hometown, you are awesome. Shot outs to Simba, Sunny, Lee, Ella, Yau, Tiffany, and the rest of the crew. Mr. Evans at Expressions, Massamba in Queens, Sepia Sand and Sable, much success to you all. I can't go on without thanking Sean. I appreciate your assistance with setting me up in a stress-free situation and thank you dearly.

Whether you've given technical, moral, or emotional support during this project, I want to thank you. If for some reason you want to give financial support, place your name here _____. SMILE.

In closing, I'd like to acknowledge my niece who is a movie director in training. Kinae, get busy, we've got to get these novels to the big screen. Jasmine, can you believe you finally got a chance to read Bruised? Now, you are the official bookseller in North Carolina- smile. To my two precious little ladies, all of this hard work is for you. You are my inspiration and reason for living. I thank you for giving my life purpose and meaning. I love you both unconditionally.

Peace,
Azarel

Also by Azárel

A Life to Remember
Bruised – Part One

**Special note
This book is a sequel.
However, it can stand alone.**

Enjoy!

Chapter
• • • • • • • • • •
1

Carlie glided down the aisle like the princess her man had been waiting on. With only the groom and the Chaplain in sight, she faked a smile like everything was perfect. The fantasy-like ceremony had her emotions on edge. On one hand, she loved Devon and felt this was the right thing to do. But something just didn't seem right.

It wasn't until the slender prison guard yelled, "Devon, you got ten minutes! Make this shit snappy!" that Carlie realized she was actually getting married in the chapel of a prison.

Devon didn't care that his bride was already nervous. "Fuck you!" he yelled. "Nigga, can't you see I'm gettin' married?"

The Chaplin cleared his throat, showing disapproval of Devon's language. "May we proceed?" he asked, peering over his glasses.

Devon blatantly ignored the Chaplin. He stared at his stylish bride briefly, then pulled her close and jammed his tongue down her throat. Although Carlie was embarrassed by his behavior, she returned the kiss with the same intense passion. She had a soft heart, and understood that Devon had been locked up for almost five years. Besides, she felt bad, knowing that she helped to convict him. But Carlie couldn't condone the way he began to grind his manhood against her body.

"That's enough, Devon!" she shouted, as she pulled away from him.

"That's enough?" he barked. Devon took on his street persona, like he was ready to go toe-to-toe with someone his own size. "You belong to me now, don't you?" His huge body invaded her space.

Instinct kicked in, and Carlie turned to see if the two correctional officers were still in the back of the room. Her adrenaline rose at a fast pace when she noticed the slender guard with his hand on his gun. Suddenly, she felt a wad of her jet-black hair being yanked by Devon's clutch. *Not again,* she thought. *This is supposed to be my wedding day.*

Devon's oversized hand gripped Carlie's left breast. She couldn't tell if her breast was under attack, or if the forceful movement was part of a massage. Instantly, Carlie snapped her neck downward for a quick look at the ring. The four-carat stone had plenty of bling, but not enough for her to withstand being in a headlock.

Within seconds, the taller of the two guards had Devon face down on the ground, with the tip of his patent-leather shoe embedded in Devon's neck. "Consider this wedding over!" he yelled.

Carlie stood back, with her hands smothering her face. "Why, Devon? Why?" she cried, as tears rolled down her smooth Caribbean-tanned skin.

While Devon was being raised up off the floor, Carlie panicked when she noticed his monstrous hand reaching for her face. She kicked and screamed like she was being attacked by pit bulls.

If it weren't for the pressure of her bladder, she wouldn't have woken up from her awful dream. Her eyes opened slightly to verify that she was home in her own bed and not in a prison. The familiar clock, given as a gift by her late grandmother, read 4:20 a.m. and verified she was indeed safe and away from Devon.

Carlie lay in bed, panting at the thought of being hit by Devon. She couldn't believe that she had dreamt of coming close to being Mrs. Devon McNeil. Instantly, she wondered if Kirk had heard any of her screams. She rolled over, praying that he was sound asleep. *He was too good of a man to lose.* Her arm patted the bed in the darkness, reaching for the feel of his skin. To her surprise, once again, he hadn't made it home yet.

Chapter
· · · · · · · · · ·
2

Hundreds of miles away, for a split second, Kirk thought about Carlie as he freaked his other woman against the wall. He felt slightly bad about being in New York, almost four hours away from home, but as the pictures fell to the floor, he continued slamming his dick into China against the wall. For now, his only goal was to make her scream. Silently, he thanked her for the way she brought the Mandingo out in him.

With Carlie he was reserved, careful not to ask for too much out of the ordinary. But with China, it was anything goes. Kirk often wondered if her wild sexual appetite came from her deceased father who was Puerto Rican, or her mother, who is Dominican.

China's mother was known to be a crazy, good-time type woman. For years she ran the streets hopping from one guy to the next in search of love. She had even met China's father when she was in the military and traveled to Beijing for her job. The one night stand produced China Hernandez, *hence the name China,* and she was now turning out to be just like her mother. From the pictures scattered on the floor, she looked like her too.

"Right there, Poppi," China growled in her Spanish accent. "Give me your pinga, baby! Fuck me!" she yelled. Kirk knew she wanted him desperately when she started mixing Spanish words with English. She did that often, but only when excited or angry. By now Kirk was familiar with the Spanish words she used often, but pinga, meaning dick, was her favorite.

All of a sudden, China ripped the last two buttons from her own shirt like a hungry lion under attack. Then stroking her fingers through his curly hair, she yanked his head toward her erect nipples.

Kirk instantly pinned both of her petite hands against the wall as they locked eyes. He stopped for a second to size up the sex monster before him. He always wondered why he was so attracted to the woman; neither her looks, nor personality compared to Carlie. China's overly-thin arched eyebrows looked like they were drawn on with a pencil, and the make-up she wore was consistently over-dramatized.

For the past two years, Kirk had been selling China a dream that someday they'd be together. Maybe it was because she was a down-ass-woman and had come from nothing, just as he had. Or maybe it was because he didn't have to act a certain way in her presence as he did with Carlie. It was clear that Kirk had never been attracted to the ghetto, low-budget type, but something about China had him hooked. He often thought about the fact that she depended on him for everything, while Carlie could no doubt make it without him.

As Kirk's mind wondered, China had thoughts of her

own, but only about feeling him inside her walls. Scanning his 280-pound frame, her eyes zoomed in on his rock-hard dick. It stood slightly above her hips, ferociously at attention.

"This pinga belongs to me, doesn't it, Poppi?" she asked, drooling over his nine-inch piece. By now, China was in heat.

Unable to wait for Kirk to make his move, she jumped on him and at the same time, grabbed what she considered hers. Wrapping her hairy legs around his waist, she bucked her hips like a wild animal.

"Fuck me, cowboy!" she yelled, while swinging her arms. Her expression begged for a rough entry, but Kirk was already aware of how she liked it. With her short, spiked, bronze-toned hair, she was *spread-eagle* on the wall, pussy open wide, resembling a victim of the exorcist. She screamed at the top of her lungs, "Oh, yeah!" as he plunged into her with fury. "That's it , baby. Work the pinga!"

As China continued to blurt out dirty remarks, Kirk wondered if the neighbors could hear. *Of course they can*, he thought, which was a complete turn-on for him. Suddenly, he positioned himself to dig deeper. With his pants slightly hanging below his knees, he was careful not to trip as he stroked China up and down the freshly painted wall.

"Talk dirty to me, Poppi!" China hollered with pleasure. Her normal tone was already high-pitched, but today the squeaky voice sounded like Rosie Perez in a horror film.

As China rode him frantically like an energetic jockey on a racehorse, Kirk thought long and hard. He couldn't think of any vulgar taunts to throw back, or any unheard of sexual acts to perform. China was a freak and liked her sex, dirty and rough, so he had to think outside the box if he wanted to keep her satisfied. They'd experimented with just about every sex toy on the market and were now into more bizarre ways to have sex.

Instantly, Kirk spun China around and tried to throw her toward the bed, but she wouldn't let go. Her body jerked as she latched on, like a determined bull rider. The moment Kirk yanked her on top of him, she went wild trying to take control. She was strong for a short, 110-pound woman, but was no match for Kirk. China grinded forcefully, and her movements were met by his increased pace. Kirk pounded like he was hired to beat the pussy up. Sweat poured and the bedpost squeaked. Worn-out, Kirk and China, at the same time released their juices and collapsed on the floor.

* * *

Three hours later, Kirk turned his sweaty body over and looked at the clock radio. *Oh shit*, he thought. He jumped from the bed with a sheet straddled between his legs and rushed to open the curtains. When the sun came shining through, he knew he had some explaining to do. His eyes searched for his cell phone, that was on vibrate. He could've sworn it was placed on top of his jacket, but for some odd reason, he couldn't find it.

Kirk had always been a quick thinker. He decided to get dressed, fight off China, and call Carlie once out the door. Before he could reach the bathroom, Miss Fatal Attraction was two steps ahead. Her threatening eyebrows creased as she leaned against the bathroom door with an unpredictable look in her eyes.

"I know you ain't leavin' me," she said, pointing her finger toward her chest. "You rushin' to be with that stuck-up-ass puta?"

Kirk hesitated and shook his head. "China, let's not get started," he said calmly. "And what the fuck is puta?"

"Bitch, whore, prostitute, or whatever you want to call her!"

"Don't I give you everything you need?" He spread his arms wide, hoping a hug would calm her.

Immediately, China smacked his hands, dismissing any chance of making up. "You been sayin' you gon' leave her for over a year now!"

"I am. I just got a lot tied up right now. If I leave her, I lose everything. *We* lose everything."

She pushed Kirk with all her might, but his body didn't budge. This scene was becoming all too familiar. "I deserve better!" Her neck rolled like an indignant woman ready to whip ass. "When somebody else is workin' this pussy, you gon' be sick!" she yelled. "Besides, you should be glad your fat-ass got a woman like me." China fingered herself slowly, and slid her scented finger across Kirk's lips.

Kirk frowned at the smell. "No doubt, but you need my fat ass. That's why you acting like this," he smirked.

Kirk's comeback was spoken in a matter-of-fact tone. China had no words to retaliate. His response was obviously too sarcastic and struck a nerve. He ducked just in time as the vase filled with old roses he'd given China came flying his way.

"Fuck you and your roses!" she screamed, at the top of her lungs. "I never wanted the mufuckas anyway. That snooty bitch got you trippin'." China's nearly white complexion was now light red. She paced the floor in front of Kirk, like she was considering an attack. "A bitch like me don't need roses, I need dick and money! Pinga, baby!"

Blowing air through her mouth, she fumed like a small child having a temper tantrum. She continued to walk back and forth, while Kirk contemplated on what to do next. He knew if he took a shower, he'd be giving her free reign to sabotage his car, cell phone, or whatever else she could get her hands on. Suddenly, he decided to skip the shower and settle for a quick wipe down.

As the water ran in the bathroom sink, Kirk quickly brushed his teeth, peeping back every other second to check on China's movements. He let his guard down as he watched her settle down in a chair near where his clothes lay. He snickered at how pathetic she looked when he noticed her rubbing his pants against her face. He figured this was her way of having something of his close to her body. At that point, Kirk felt comfortable enough to close the bathroom door momentarily for a little bit of privacy.

As soon as China heard the door shut, she leaped into action. "What a fool," she mumbled. Grabbing Kirk's cell phone from inside the sofa cushion, she smiled, knowing that he had never found it. She scrolled through the numbers quickly. Most of the missed calls displayed code names. *Probably his hoochies*, she thought. But Carlie's number was evident. Her missed calls showed up like clockwork. *3:00 a.m., 4:00 a.m., man, she's so pressed*, China thought. She had to laugh to herself at her next thought when looking at the 5:30 missed call. *Umh...just as he was gettin' his last nut.*

All at once, the water stopped running and China pressed delete, delete, delete. "Be gone, freak." She snickered, amused by her childish actions.

China became nervous when she heard Kirk's voice.

"China, bring my stuff in here."

"What's in it for me?" she asked, smacking her lips between words.

He smiled, knowing how to make her happy. "Look in my pant's pocket and grab five hundreds."

"Nigga, I ain't no pipe head," she snapped.

"That's all I got for now. There's more where that came from later."

Kirk hated giving her that much money during rough times. The streets hadn't been good to him lately, so he really needed to hold on to every dollar in his pocket. The real problem was that Kirk wasn't really the thug type. He wanted to be, but it wasn't truly in him. So, he didn't make the same money that other guys selling drugs did. Which meant China needed to back off.

She smacked her lips with disgust as the sound of water flowing from the faucet started again. "I'll fix him." China jetted across the room and grabbed her soiled animal-printed thongs from off the floor. Balling the string-like garment up, she grinned while stuffing it inside Kirk's leather bomber jacket.

"Anythin' else, Poppi?" she yelled, watching the bathroom door closely.

"Nah, just my pants and T-shirt."

"Okay, be right there," she responded innocently.

China had one more trick up her sleeve. She rummaged through several of her make-up cases, looking for the brightest red lipstick she could find. She wanted to make sure Carlie would notice the lipstick imprint on Kirk's wife beater. Within seconds, China worked the lipstick heavily across her lips. Then, taking hold of the T-shirt near the bottom, she puckered up and kissed the shirt several times, leaving an imprint of her luscious lips. Then she sashayed across the room like the happy housewife, just as Kirk called out her name.

"China, what's taking you so long?"

"Here you go," she said, entering the bathroom.

Kirk turned to make sure she didn't have a knife. He'd been tricked by her bi-polar personality before.

"Did you get your loot?" he asked, grabbing her arms to check for weapons. After feeling nothing but the T-shirt, his sweater and jeans, he relaxed.

"Got it." She smiled. "Do you really have to go right this minute? I was gon' fix us some breakfast." China pulled slightly away from his grip and turned his face away from hers. "Let me help you with your T-shirt." She couldn't believe Kirk was that stupid. Before she knew it, the shirt was pulled over his head, and the lipstick imprint lay perfectly and colorful on the lower back of his shirt.

"All set, just throw your sweater on so you can jet. Oh yeah, here's your phone," she said, handing it to him with a grin.

Several minutes later, Kirk was headed down the steps of China's Brownstone on West 127th Street. The block was hot with people walking the streets of Harlem, as if the day hadn't just begun. It was apparent that his black leather coat did more for his image than keep him warm. He shivered and checked the block for Carlie's private investigators, before making his way to his new 600 Mercedes Benz. Just as he tapped the button on the keys to the car alarm, China appeared in her doorway. Wearing a skimpy two-piece pajama set, she bit into an apple and waved casually, allowing anyone passing by to see her.

Kirk shouted, "Get back in the house!" He checked to see if anybody was stealing a quick look at his woman.

China grinned devilishly and disappeared from the doorway. Although Kirk appeared to be jealous, she knew he was dying to get away to call Carlie. She thought about making a few calls of her own. Why let Kirk have his cake and eat it too? She was entitled to a little extra sex too? Maybe giving Kirk a taste of his own medicine was what he needed.

Her first thought was to call Mike, the fine mixed brotha she'd met over a month ago. She wasn't sure whether it was his half-Dominican side, or his black origin that made him so damn crazy.

She thought back to their fourth date. Just when things were moving in the right direction for them, she showed up at his house one night for a big surprise. He'd asked her to come over in her sexist attire, ready for a night full of fun. China took that as a sign that she was special. Special enough that he'd planned something romantic. She'd never gotten that from a guy before. They always wanted to hit and run.

So, China dressed up in her sexiest gear, thinking a romantic night was ahead. Only minutes after arriving did she realize the party wasn't just for the two of them. Mike had actually arranged for his boy to be there and share China's goodies. Needless to say, she remembered leaving there doing a hundred. She knew people thought of her as being wild and loving rough sex, but she only wanted it from one man. The thought of Mike's crazy ass, made her realize that Kirk wasn't so bad after all. Out of all of her crazy experiences, he had treated her best.

She peeked from the window one last time just before he

pulled off. *My man,* she thought.

As soon as Kirk hopped in and started the car, he grabbed the cell to call Carlie. Checking the calls, he wondered why she hadn't called. He thought for sure that by now, she would've been upset that he'd stayed out all night. Late nights were normal for Kirk, but never when they weren't pre-planned. And surely an all-nighter wasn't acceptable. He called her several times, but still no answer from Carlie. Kirk thought about hitting the highway to head home, but first needed to check on his runners before leaving New York.

Approaching the 8 o'clock rush hour, he hopped into traffic and cruised toward St. Nicks Projects. While the beats of Lil John blasted through the upgraded Bose system, Kirk couldn't help but to think about his financial situation. At thirty-four years old, he was starting to feel like a failure. He'd spent the majority of his late twenties following behind his boy, Devon, like a flunky. Then, after making a cut-throat move, and taking Devon's woman, he still ended up half-broke and buying grams instead of kilos from someone else.

At times he wondered what was it that made Devon so successful? He'd followed the same pattern, gave his clients good prices, and hired no-nonsense workers. But considering that he could only sneak to New York once or twice a week, Kirk had to strongly rely on his main-man Snake. When the product would run low, he'd do his best to replenish the stash, and Snake was always good for the money.

Although he was bringing in a decent amount of cash, it didn't compare to the money Carlie was making. Fresh out of law school, she was raking in $150 an hour, roughly $24,000 a month as a criminal attorney. Her father, Ricky Stewart, had laid the foundation, and made sure that her office received the appropriate business. Carlie never bragged on her situation, but she expected Kirk to be a go-getter and do something positive with his life. She made it very clear that, no drug dealing men would be involved in her life ever again.

In no time, Kirk had pulled up to 135th and St. Nicholas Avenue. Flashbacks of how he'd been wasting his life had sidetracked him a bit. He sat patiently in his car, waiting for Snake to appear in the upstairs window. As usual, the lookout would notice him and make the call to Snake. Phone calls to Snake were absolutely forbidden. If there was one thing he'd learned from Devon was that a taped conversation would be the easiest way to get sent upstate. He tried to stop thinking so hard and focus on the business ahead of him.

Before he knew it, Snake opened the car door and slid in. At that same moment, Carlie was ringing his phone. He answered on the first ring, like everything was normal.

"What's up, pretty lady?" He looked over at Snake, shooting him a look that said, *don't say a word.*

"What's up?" she asked, in a lady-like manner. "I want to know why I haven't heard from you all night?" Carlie was careful not to start an argument right before walking into her office. "I can't take this too much longer. Now I know you're trying to build your car business, but if this is what things are going to be like, let's end this now!" Carlie spoke with authority, like she was the head honcho in the relationship.

"See, I'm just tryna make a decent living for us, and look what I get." Kirk turned slightly to check Snake's reaction. He certainly didn't want to seem like a sucker in front of the hired help. "You're so right. I should've called," he agreed, in an attempt to get Carlie off the phone. "But after 3 a.m., I just figured I'd let you sleep. I'm here right now with the guy who's releasing the car. So I'll be hitting the highway in a few."

"What kinda car did you buy?" she asked, throwing Kirk a curve ball. Her four-year law school training made this a natural instinct for her.

He stuttered. "It…it…it's a 1997 Camry."

"You got a buyer already?"

"Not yet. I think I'll put it in the paper this week." He rambled on for several minutes, before Carlie's interrogation ended. "I'll be home before you get off," he said.

"You wanna do something for me? Sell that damn car! I'm not thrilled about taking care of grown men!" Click.

"Damn," he mouthed to himself, as he leaned back in the seat. "That was work. I gotta take home something special."

"Nigga, you still got your girl thinkin' you a car sales-man?" Snake laughed, like he was at a comedy show. The gold tooth in his mouth shined brighter, the more he made fun of his boss. "Yeah, I forgot…she gon' kick yo ass to the curb when she find out you still a street nigga, a strugglin' one at that." By now, Snake was doubled over in the seat. He was always extra animated and acted more like a teenager than a twenty-one year old.

Kirk looked over at Snake and held his hand out. He wanted to kick his short, stocking-cap wearing employee out of the car. Instead, he quickly counted the five thousand dol-lars and pressed unlock on the doors, signaling the Lil-Wayne look-alike to get out.

Chapter
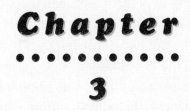
3

Carlie strutted toward her downtown office in the heart of Boston, Massachusetts. Her thick, long succulent legs had the streets buzzing with excitement. Every step she took caused men to stop in their tracks for a salivating stare. Even men with women by their sides couldn't resist giving up a slight glance.

As soon as she opened the wide glass doors to her building, the sexy bald-headed guard couldn't resist saying something. "Damn, Ms. Carlie," he growled. "You gotta stop comin' in here looking like that. A brotha can't work under these conditions."

Carlie lifted her shades slightly and laughed. "Good morning to you too," she responded.

Dressed in a silver $2,200 St. Johns suit, she stood in front of the elevator like a super model and greeted everyone who crossed her path. Although she possessed a slender build, Carlie had actually gained a little weight since moving to Massachusetts. But to those who watched her closely, it was all in the right places.

Just as she stepped off the elevator and headed toward the brass sign that read, Stewart and Associates, she was instantly greeted by her hyperactive secretary, Jewell.

"Ms. Stewart, I sure am glad you're here," she ranted, while trailing Carlie like a lost puppy. "It's kinda strange for you to sleep in...I expected you here earlier. Are you okay?" Jewell spoke a mile a minute. "The phones have been ringing off the hook. Your father called and said to call him as soon as you..."

"Jewell, I need a moment," she said, stopping her in her tracks. "If it's not life-threatening, it can wait." Carlie tried pushing the hardwood door to her office shut, but Jewell's hand slipped through, stopping it from closing. "What is it Jewell?" she asked, in a condescending tone.

"You might want this letter now."

"Thanks. Sit it on my desk."

"You look mighty pretty today," she said, sitting the letter down.

Carlie shot her a cold stare and left the envelope on the corner of her desk. She wondered how she'd make it through the day. After a long, sleepless night, and now tons of work ahead of her, she leaned back in her high leather-back chair and relaxed.

She knew her father would be calling soon to check on the Dupree case. This particular case had Carlie on edge for weeks. She hadn't anticipated on having so much involvement with clients and families when she decided to become a criminal lawyer. However, just five months after graduation, she was as deep into her profession as P. Diddy was in the music business.

The Dupree case was the most publicized case the city of
Boston had seen in years. With Ricky's influence, as soon as
Marcus Dupree was locked up for allegedly shooting his girlfriend, his family contacted Stewart and Associates immediately. Although Carlie had only tried two other criminal cases
on her own, she vowed to give this one her all. Two things
were in her favor, one, her father called for a phone conference from Maryland weekly to provide guidance, and two,
she truly believed her client did not do it.

Winning the case was equally as important as doing
everything else the right way. Ricky Stewart was already
established as a prominent attorney, so people looked to
Carlie to follow in her father's footsteps, both in and out of
the courtroom. Not to mention that her father stayed on her
about her relationship with Kirk. *I'm sure you're starting to
plan the wedding,* he would say.

Ricky Stewart was so happy that Carlie had finally found
herself a working man. Even though his life was rolling at full
speed and in another state, he made it his business to talk to
his daughter often about her relationship. It was important
for him to see Carlie with the right man, and he vowed to do
whatever it took to make sure she was treated right.

On many occasions, he knew he was overstepping his
boundaries by fighting his daughter's battles, but that's just
what the Stewarts do. Carlie frowned a bit as she reminisced
about the time her father was shot at because of her. Ricky
ended up in the middle of a shoot-out at a funeral parlor
with some of Devon's flunkies. He hated going toe-to-toe
with youngsters, but he couldn't have gangstas threatening
his daughter. In the end, he ended up splattering a nineteen-
year-old dead to the ground, all to keep his baby from harm.

As soon as the phone rang, Carlie snapped from her daze and scrambled for the Dupree folder. She figured the call was for her. Upon spotting it, her eyes instantly became glued to the letter Jewell had brought in. Carlie's heart rate tripled. The excitement she felt inside had her twisted. Seeing his name brought back memories, both good and bad.

She held the letter in the palm of her hand, studying the handwriting. *Devon McNeil* appeared in the upper left hand corner, *no return address*. Carlie hesitated and let out a huge sigh before ripping the envelope.

> Carlie,
>
> I know this letter finds you well and sexy, no doubt. I've searched all over for your where-abouts. I ended up spendin' money that I don't have to locate you. I'm so proud of you. We did it! My folks tell me sometimes you're even on the news. Damn, girl, you doin' the damn thing. That's my girl. You deserve it. As a matter of fact, you deserve everything you've ever wanted in life. And you definitely deserve to be pampered by a man, but not just any man, me! Every time I look at your picture, your light bronze complexion gives me a hard-on. I haven't been with a woman in five years, so you know you in trouble when I see you.

Carlie squirmed in her seat at the thought of Devon talking to her that way. All of the good times they shared rushed to the forefront of her mind, especially their sex life. Light sweat formed all over her body. She folded the letter slightly, to savor the words her eyes had taken in. Flashbacks of Devon's hungry kisses, and him feasting on her toes all the way up to her clit had her spellbound. She sat frozen at the thought of him removing her satin, silver thongs. Jewell's voice on the speakerphone shattered any hopes of her continuing to fantasize about Devon.

"It's the new investigator, on Line 2," Jewell said.

Carlie slammed her finger on the button as fast as she could. "Take a message and hold all calls, even my father," she said, in a frenzy. Carlie's eyes darted back to the letter.

To this day, I can't recall everything that happened between us, but I know that I still want you, and I'm gonna make things right. Tell all those fly-by-night niggas that you about to get back with yo man, especially Kirk. Better yet, give him this message. I owe him one. Maybe even three. That's one to the head and two to the body. Yeah, I know about that flaky-ass nigga. I've got eyes and ears everywhere. Tell'em we'll meet again real soon. And you watch out for that pussy fiend, he got bitches everywhere.

Peace,

Devon, Your #One Man

21

After reading the letter, Carlie was halfway frightened and halfway excited. A part of her still had feelings for Devon, but knew that he wasn't the man for her. Besides, her father would be livid if she went backwards. Of course, she didn't have too much to worry about because Devon was locked up and could only send letters.

Instantly, Carlie looked back at the envelope. *No return address,* she thought. We'll meet again soon. *What does he mean by that?* Her mind raced. She thought back to his sentencing day, over four and a half years ago. On one count, thirty-seven years to life, and one life sentence on the count of drug conspiracy. He can't be getting out!

The contents of the letter had her both alarmed and mixed up. Carlie kicked off her $800 Giuseppe shoes and headed toward the plush sofa. She had no intention of working under that type of pressure, even though the Duprees paid her a $15,000 retainer fee.

Stretched out on the couch, thoughts ran through Carlie's mind like the Concord headed to Paris. She couldn't believe she was having romantic thoughts about Devon. After all, he had left her emotionally bruised, and whipped her ass every time things didn't go his way. She thought back to over five years ago when she was laid up in the hospital with fractured ribs, and severe cuts and bruises beneath her eyes. She remembered so clearly how Devon had whipped her like she was his worst enemy. Then, a day later, apologized like the beating meant nothing.

With Kirk, she didn't have to worry about him putting his hands on her. He was more of a gentleman, and had been raised to never strike a woman. But mentally, sexually or emotionally, he wasn't ringing any bells. Sex with Kirk was quick and spiritless. Half the time she would lay stiff, or pretend to be wound-up about his unexciting orgasm. She thought about how she suffered many nights on all fours, pretending to enjoy Kirk's favorite position.

On occasions, she tried sexy lingerie, and nights out on the town, to bring some spark to their relationship. After all, this was the man who gave up his life and followed her to Massachusetts, and if this was the man she was going to marry, she needed to make this work.

Ricky was counting on her to have a normal life, with a husband, children, a successful career, the whole nine yards. Day by day she prayed that things would work out, and that she'd learn to love Kirk. Which made her wonder why Devon would refer to Kirk in his letter as a pussy fiend. Was Kirk cheating on her? How would Devon know anyway? They say news travels through prisons faster than it does on the streets. Be that as it may, Carlie rationalized the situation by deciding that Kirk compensated for his lack of sexual excitement by being a real man, with a real job, without handcuffs, something Devon couldn't compete with.

The emotional stress had her traumatized, with way too many memories in one day. Carlie grabbed the remote and pressed the button to close the drapes near her desk. She needed a few minutes of peace, no sunlight, no thoughts of Devon or Kirk, just rest. She balled the letter up, threw it across the room and closed her eyes.

* * *

As the door opened, Carlie was asleep and deep into dream mode. She tossed and turned, as if she were home in the comfort of her own bed. With one leg thrown over the bottom wedge of the couch, her body gyrated up and down.

Rotating from right to left, her head acted like a stiff robot being kissed all over. As the footsteps moved closer, she moaned, "Yes, yes…" The moisture from her body caused her skin to glisten. *Irresistible*, he thought, standing directly above her.

"Don't stop," Carlie mumbled, in a sexy tone.

The insatiable sound caused Kirk to think fast. He doubled back and locked the doors to her office. Once again, he stood above Carlie with two champagne flutes, a chilled bottle of Veuve Clicquot, and a royal blue jewelry box. His initial plan was to make things right with Carlie by surprising her with a small daytime treat, but this opportunity was so much better. *She always said she wanted spontaneity in our relationship*, he thought.

Kirk placed the jewelry box to his left near the champagne and knelt just below Carlie's belly-button. As soon as he began his fondling, Carlie's breathing intensified. The first touch made her think about the last time she saw Devon's chiseled body, but the first lick made her scream.

"Oh, Devon!" she hollered.

"Devon? What the fuck?" Kirk shouted, in a state of rage.

Hearing Kirk's voice instantly woke Carlie from her sleep. "Kirk," she said nervously. "What are you doin' here?" Carlie fumbled with her skirt and bra, making sure everything was in place. She had no idea that her actions and thoughts were completely transparent. All she knew was that her panties were soaked.

"You dreaming about some nigga who kicked your ass and constantly left you with bruises!" Kirk moved across the room, thinking about his next move. His offensive expression showed that he was about to blow his cool.

Carlie shot him a guilty response. "Who?"

"Who? Don't ask me no stupid shit like that. Who's fucking name did you call out?"

Carlie had been taught how to play it to the end. Had he really heard her call out Devon's name? "Oh, that's real good, Kirk. Take the focus off of you. You're the one staying out all night."

"I'm doing this for us. I'm tryna be what you want me to be, a nine-to- five nigga. So, I gotta make this car selling shit work."

"Yeah, right! It doesn't take all night to buy and sell a car. I'm far from stupid."

"Check this. You're stupid 'cause you used to let Devon physically fuck you up, and now you in here letting him mentally fuck you!"

"He may have abused me physically, but guess what? Now you're abusing me mentally. I'm not happy, Kirk! I'm tired of sleeping with a gun to protect me in the middle of the night."

"You choose to sleep with that gun under the bed. I'm not gone that often."

"Are you seeing somebody?" she blurted out.

"Why would you ask me something like that?" Kirk's entire expression changed. He couldn't afford for Carlie to kick him to the curb. She was his ticket to officially coming off the streets. If she gave him the $200,000 he needed to start his dealership, he'd be set in years to come and could be with China if he wanted to. He had given Carlie the business plan over two weeks ago, but hadn't pressured her into committing thus far.

"Let's just say a little birdie told me," Carlie finally answered, with a doubtful attitude.

Without delay, Kirk pulled his wallet out and flipped through the tiny compartments. "Look Carlie, I've really been trying to please you. I've even been approved for my dealer license." Kirk searched for the paper like he was looking for a winning lottery ticket. "Where the hell is it?" he yelled, in a panic. "Carlie, it was here…" He glanced at her scowl. He knew she didn't believe him, but there was nothing he could do about it. Not only was the paper missing, but Carlie's social security card too!

Kirk panicked, remembering that Carlie never wanted to give up her cards anyway. The only reason she gave in was because Kirk needed to show the small-time dealer where he bought the Benz, a copy of Carlie's social security card. He had already taken her Visa and imprinted the card, for the down payment days before. For some strange reason, the Visa was still in the wallet but the social security card was missing.

Out of the blue, Kirk's head turned from side to side like he was looking for something. He knew his papers, nor Carlie's card was in her office, but suddenly his eyes focused on the crumbled up paper on the floor. As he reached for it, Carlie covered her face.

"It's not what it seems," she pleaded.

"Guilty already?" he questioned.

Carlie sat back and shook her head. *Busted,* she thought.

Chapter
• • • • • • • • • • •
4

Carlie paced back and forth. "What do you mean, I turned it off?" She spoke into the handset with a high-pitched voice, as if she had a personal vendetta with the cordless phone.

At this point, she hadn't lost her cool, but was without a doubt on the verge of filing a lawsuit.

"Miss, get this, I use my cell phone for work, and right now I'm missing some very important phone calls." Her index finger pointed across the room, like she was directing her comments to a physical body. She meant business, and her tone verified it.

"Ms. Stewart, we only did what you instructed us to do," the Nextel representative responded politely. "You told us to disconnect the service."

"I'm telling you, this must be a mistake! I thought you had to have my information to turn my phone off?" Carlie was nearly burning a hole in the carpet.

"Yes, the notes on the account show that your address and

social security number were given to access the account."

The line beeped. "Can I put you on hold for just a second?"

"Sure."

Click. "Hello."

Ricky's dominate voice blasted through the line. "Carlie, what's going on? I've been calling you for two days, trying to discuss the Dupree case. "And why aren't you in the office, we have a business to run!"

"I know, Dad. My cell phone has been turned off by mistake. Can I call you right back? I have the rep on the line."

"Certainly. But if I don't hear from you shortly, I will be calling you back."

Click. "Okay, so what do I need to do at this point?" she asked, returning to the line. Carlie's head snapped toward the door, she thought she heard a knock.

"Provide your address and social security number, and we can get you re-connected in the next hour or so."

"Hour!"

"Yes, that's the best I can do. Also, there will be a re-connect fee."

Carlie said nothing as the knock on the door got louder. It was almost as if she were running a three-ring circus. From the knocks at the door, and the numerous calls, she was going crazy.

"Where's your key," she mouthed, as she opened the door for Kirk.

"I must've misplaced my house keys," he whispered, realizing she was on a call. The closer he got to Carlie the more she got a whiff of his strong cologne and freshly showered smell. She looked at his casual attire and wondered where he'd been. He always dressed more mature than other guys she'd dated, but something was suspicious.

Carlie sat on the extra-large lounging chair, with her head held low, as the woman ran down the policy and completed the transaction. Kirk entered the living room sensing her frustration. He slid his hands beneath her long, hair and attempted to rub the stress from her shoulders. As he straddled her from behind, Carlie was a bit standoffish, but when the phone beeped again, it gave her a chance to move away.

"Ma'am, would you mind holding one last time?"

"Uh-huh," the woman responded, as if she was sick of being placed on hold.

Click. "Carlie!" Jewell shouted. "The credit card company called the office. They said someone has been ordering all of these clothes and charging it to your Visa! At first I thought it was you, until they said the stuff was being sent to New York!"

"Calm down, Jewell. I'll take care of it as soon as I get off the other line. I gotta call you back!" Carlie knew she had to stay calm.

Click. "Okay, are we done?" she asked the rep, in a snappy tone. "Now someone is making charges on my credit card!"

"I'm sorry to hear that, Ms. Stewart. And yes, I'm done. Is there anything else I can do for you?"

"No."

"Thanks for calling, Nextel."

By now, Kirk's mouth was as wide as a shark on a hungry day. It was all becoming clear. The missing dealers license, Carlie's social security card and Visa card had all been in his wallet the day before. He knew China had pulled a fast one somehow. He had to take Carlie's mind off the situation until he could get hold of China and rectify the situation.

Kirk hopped up and ran into the bedroom. Within seconds, he was back holding the same jewelry box as he had the day before. This time he didn't give life a chance to keep her from opening it.

"Bam," he said, in a wimpy tone.

"Oh, that's nice," Carlie responded unimpressed. She stared at the eight-inch diamond tennis bracelet like it was nothing. She wouldn't even touch it.

Kirk held the box open starting to feel like she didn't want it. "It's for you," he said jokingly.

"I know. Thanks."

Kirk still held the box in his hand. "Aren't you gonna try it on?"

"Can I try it on later, Kirk? I'm so pissed right now."

The phone rang again. "I've got to answer to my father right now," she said, grabbing the phone. "Hello, Dad." Carlie whined like she had zero energy left to talk.

"Yeah, I got yo mufuckin' Dad, a'ight!" the irate voice said.

Carlie breathed long and hard. She couldn't handle all of the drama coming head-on in one day. "Who is this?" she asked, as she gritted her teeth.

"This is the bitch who is takin' yo man."

Carlie's eyes darted over to Kirk, whose eyes were wide open. He dropped the box, knowing trouble was on the phone. "What is it, Carlie?" he asked hesitantly.

"I just want you to know that when you lookin' for the man you lying wit' from time to time, when he's missing, you can find him between my legs!" the female on the phone said.

Carlie wasn't about to let some ghetto hoe take her outside of her character, she had way more class than that. "I tell you what, he's here now." She spoke clearly and enunciated each word. "If he wants you, he's free to go. I'll put him on," she said, with a confident look on her face. Although Carlie was bothered by the call, and the fact that another woman had her phone number, she wasn't about to let her think she had ruffled her feathers at all. "Here you go, Kirk!" she yelled in his direction.

Kirk certainly didn't want to be put out of a luxury home to live in New York with China. Besides, he needed Carlie to front him some money, and fast. "Hell no, I'm not getting on the damn phone!" He ranted and yelled even louder, like he was telling the truth. "Whoever it is, they lying, playing games and shit!"

Carlie placed the phone back to her ear. China had gone ballistic. She spoke a combination of Spanish, Dominican, and Puerto Rican mixed with English every other sentence. She blended her curse words from different languages so well, like she knew exactly what she wanted to say. Carlie had learned a little bit of Spanish over the years and knew that when China yelled, "Hacer la sopa," she was telling her to lick her pussy. Puta, cutrue, and capullo, were words Carlie couldn't figure out, but she understood that she was being cursed out royally. Finally, after minutes, the verbal assault stopped completely.

"I tell you what," China said, in a deranged voice, as if she had changed personalities. "Check his black leather jacket. When he was here the other night, I stuffed a lil' treat for you in his inside pocket."

Carlie's brow puckered. She thought about telling Kirk

what China said. Instead, she jetted to the closet and grabbed the jacket. Kirk was close on her heels, but he was still too late. As she dangled the animal printed panties in the air, his heart sunk.

"You lying bastard!" Carlie yelled.

China enjoyed hearing the news. "You can have those," she joked. "Most of the time, I just go without! You can never say China ain't done nothin' for you." She laughed hysterically.

Carlie hung up and began to cry. She thought about how her life was supposed to be near perfect at this point. She hadn't shed a tear since the Devon days, and now she was letting some tramp take her back there.

"Let me explain, Carlie." Kirk's face read *guilty*. "It's not what it seems." He reached for her hand, but was stopped by a smack over his right palm.

"Get out!" she hollered, pointing to the door.

"C'mon now, let's talk about this."

"I've had enough talking for one day. Call China!" she ended, pushing him toward the door.

At first, Kirk refused to leave, until Carlie swung like a wild schoolgirl. He knew she was hurt and let her hits go without a payback punch, until she seemed to be aiming for his nuts. She went wild.

"You dirty motherfucker! I trusted you!"

While Kirk fought off the hits, a part of him glared into thin air. He remembered a scene from his childhood where his mother fought off his drunken father.

In the worn down kitchen, he stood as a young boy, watching his petite mother get hammered by the back of his father's huge fist. He thought about the pain in his mother's eyes and grabbed at Carlie's arms. He shook her slightly, begging for the scuffle to end.

"I don't wanna do this," he said firmly.

"You shoulda thought about that well before now!"

Kirk shook his head. He didn't expect Carlie to understand. He had never told her that, by the time he was fifteen, his mother had died from one of his father's brutal beatings. From that moment on, he vowed to never hit a woman.

Although he'd inherited non-abusive traits because of what he'd seen his mother go through, he did pick up his father's cheating ways.

He had been dealing with China for over two years, and never understood why. He knew Carlie was a good woman, and wanted the best for him, he just couldn't keep his pants up. He thought about how Carlie was feeling and knew she needed some space. For now, he backed away giving them both time to think. He especially needed time to think of a lie.

As soon as the door shut, Kirk's phone rang. *Unknown, it's gotta be that bitch, China,* he thought. "What the fuck…?" he screamed, into his cell.

"Yo, dog, you musta had a hell'uva night!" Snake joked. "Nigga, put that shit aside, 'cause you got a problem."

"Shoot, I'm listening. What is it?"

"Yo dog, Rico told me to call you. He said some nigga that you turned against is creepin' 'round askin' questions 'bout you!"

"Who is it?"

"How the hell would I know, dog? I'm just the messenger. You know Rico don't talk on phones. He said he got caught up with you once before, but it ain't happenin' no more."

Kirk breathed a heavy sigh into the phone, but no words could express his frightening thoughts.

"Word on the street is…so much is goin' around. Are you kickin' it with some nigga's girl, or do you owe a big bill? 'Cause nothin' else would make a nigga act like that." He spoke as if this was all a big joke. Nothing was ever serious to him.

"I'll hit you back," Kirk said. He hung up, unlocked the door to his Benz, and plopped in the seat like he'd just heard the worst news in years.

Chapter

5

Like he belonged there, Devon strutted into the busy housing complex with his hands deep in his pockets. As he walked, no one paid attention to the fact that he didn't have a coat on in the middle of November, nor did they notice the bulge beneath his Roc-a-Wear T-shirt. The homemade doo-rag covered his fresh cut and met his dark shades at the crease of his brow. Resembling a two hundred and something pound bodybuilder, he shuffled back and forth near the gated basketball court, hunting his target.

To his left stood a group of low-level drug-dealers, pretending to be hanging out, while two black cops walked the beat carelessly only four feet away. Devon decided to cross the street to map out the rest of his plan, knowing that right on schedule his man would appear. On a mission, he waited patiently for the right moment to settle the score.

Realizing that nothing came free in life, he began to search for someone who looked like they needed to make a few bucks. Instantly, his eyes zoomed in on a skinny boy with thick braids, who looked to be in his early teens. Devon walked pass the boy, who was in the middle of a free-style rap battle with his friends.

He whispered, "You wanna make some money, young blood?"

"Hell yeah," the youngster responded, with energy.

"Me too!" one of the others yelled.

"Nah, all I need is one," Devon said firmly. "Come with me."

Devon led the way and the youngster followed, like he'd done this many times before. Then suddenly he stopped and asked, "How much do I get?"

Without hesitation, Devon grabbed the boy by his collar and dragged him into a deserted stairwell. He pressed his body against the boy's, allowing him to feel the hardness of the pistol.

"It's good pay! You okay with that, aren't you?"

The boy looked up at Devon with scary eyes. "Yeah, I'm good."

The thought of having to use a gun never crossed the boy's mind. He figured he'd have to pass off a package or look out for 5.0, just as he did for other guys in the hood. This seemed to be more than he bargained for.

"Here's the deal. In about five minutes, a black SUV will roll up across the street." As Devon went into his pocket, the boy's heart thumped. "When you see the short Columbian dude exit the car, hand'em this." Devon slapped the large, folded brown envelope smothered in extra tape into the boy's hand. "I'll be directly across the street. Tell'em somebody owes him that."

"That's it?" the boy asked, in a high-pitch voice.

"Yeah, I'll be standin' on this side of the street. I'll shoot you a nod to make sure you handin' it to the right guy. Oh, and this for you." Devon handed over a crisp fifty-dollar bill.

"Man, that's it?"

"Yeah. Now get your lil' ass back out there with your friends. And remember he's watchin' you."

"Who?" The boy had a confused look on his face.

Devon patted his gun and grinned. "He is."

Minutes later, the boy, with the package concealed under his shirt, was back on the block shooting the breeze with his boys. Just as the black SUV rolled up, he shot Devon a semi-frightening look. Devon stood calmly on the sidewalk, biting into a Hershey's chocolate bar as he gave the silent go-ahead.

Headed across the street the boy felt queasy. Somehow, this wasn't as easy as he thought. To make matters worse, as soon as his foot stepped onto the curb, the described target was emerging from the truck. Without hesitation, he walked up, closed his eyes, and handed the guy the package. The sounds of the guns clicking all around startled him. Three huge gangsta type dudes looked for a signal from Rico to decide what to do. They realized the boy looked harmless, but wanted answers as to why he was there. Big Tex, Rico's most trusted friend and employee, had Rico's back as he reached for the envelope.

"What is this?" Rico spoke, in his Columbian accent. He rubbed the envelope between his fingers, noticing that it felt like money.

The boy had closed his eyes after hearing the clicking sound of the gun and never opened them back up. "I don't know," he said, blinking nervously. "The guy across the street told me to give it to you."

Rico's eyes shot across the street and expanded to the size of an eight-ball. In the midst of the crowded sidewalk, he couldn't believe he spotted the light-skinned muscular man that he'd put a contract on over four years ago. Glancing back at the envelope, his mind raced. He ripped the tape off the envelope and rubbed his fingers across a few of the hundreds. While his workers watched his hands intensely, his diamond watch stood out, which had enough ice on it to cool off a glass of hot cocoa.

Instantly, he pushed the money back inside and headed across the street. Like an automatic reflex, his boys trailed him, until he threw up his hand signaling them to stop.

"I'm okay," he stated, knowing that Devon was there to pay his debt.

Removing his shades with one hand, and grabbing his gun with the other, Devon prepared for war. Although his expression made it clear that there was no fear, he was puzzled by Rico's stance.

Three feet away stood the man he owed, respected and betrayed. Now, in his early forties, Rico still wore a goatee and his smooth skin looked as if he had just come from a tanning salon. "So where do we go from here?" Devon asked bluntly.

"You call it. What's this supposed to do?" Rico asked, holding the envelope in the air.

"That's $10,000 to start. It covers your contract on me, which obviously nobody could execute." He smirked slightly. "There's more to come. Let's call it reparation fees for all the unnecessary bull-shit I've put you through."

Rico nodded. "You gotta lot of balls comin' here. What is it you really want?"

"I need to make some money. I can't do it in Maryland, too many snitches, but I trust you. What better place to come than New York? Besides, I got another beef to settle, and I hear he's out here wasting space on the block. Only I don't owe him money, he gets a bullet!"

"Main man, who you talkin' 'bout?"

"Don't play games? You know who I'm talkin' 'bout."

"Whoa….I have nothin' to do with that."

"That's cool. I can respect that." Devon nodded and twitched his lips at the same time. "It's my beef. I can handle it alone. But word is, the nigga is sellin' for you. So if I plan on doin' the nigga, I wanna go 'head and make up for the money you gonna lose. Besides, I heard he ain't puttin' too much loot in your pocket anyway." He looked for confirmation from Rico. "He ain't no real street nigga, he's more like my office assistant."

Rico stood in amazement. Devon was very serious and he knew it. He was admitting that he planned on taking Kirk out, but wanted to replace the money Rico would lose from not having Kirk around. The idea was completely crazy to Rico, but from the deranged look in Devon's eyes, he washed the entire situation.

"Let's get in the truck and talk," Rico ordered. "You look cold. Why don't you take a bit of this money back and get a coat?"

Devon snapped. "Warriors don't get cold! I'm here to do business!"

Rico's neck popped back. "You better calm down, main man." He spoke calmly, wondering where Devon picked up the extra courage toward him. "Maybe you busted off on a few cats in prison, and that's why you're so disgruntled, but keep in mind, ain't shit changed!"

Although Rico's tone only changed slightly, Devon understood what he meant. He would pop Rico if necessary, but for now, he needed him.

"Listen man, I crushed every nigga that got in my way while in the joint. I only had to pop two fake ballers." He grinned like he was amusing himself. "They tried to hustle a hustler. But you straight, and I owe you for life." He held his hand out for Rico to return the pound.

Hesitantly, Rico showed him some love. He didn't fully trust Devon, or for that matter anybody. But he did believe Devon could make him a lot of money.

"So, give me the details on how you got out. You know people gonna come up with their own stories, but I wanna hear it from the horse's mouth."

"Tell 'em to see me with all questions," Devon boasted.

"What really happened?" Rico asked, making it clear that he wanted answers.

"Man, I got smart and got me a Jewish boy for an attorney. He went back through my old documents and found out that the prosecutor, judge and district attorney, were all tryna fuck me." Devon pounded one fist into the other. "Those mufuckas was in cahoots together. When I initially signed my plea agreement, the prosecution wasn't supposed to ask for life. It was sealed in ink."

"Ahh..." Rico said, realizing he'd heard enough. "Look, man, I'm gonna be honest. You got probation watching you like a hawk. If you get caught, are you ready to take all of the heat?"

"No doubt. I know I gotta handle mine. You ain't gotta worry 'bout your name comin' up in nothin'."

"I got your word?"

"Word," Devon responded, with confidence.

Rico moved his head back and forth, as he slipped into deep thought. Something didn't seem right. *How did he find him in New York City?* For a quick moment, he thought about Devon trying to get back at him. Everyone wanted to get next to him, and that's why he didn't trust anybody. Then quickly, Rico made a decision. He knew Devon was about making money. *Maybe he was just being paranoid as usual.*

"Look, man, I'm gonna do this for the both of us. One, I know you a money makin' stallion. And two, you're right, these other jokers don't work fast like they should." Rico's voice grew deeper and firmer. "But don't cross me, 'cause trust me when I say you'll regret it!"

"Man, I won't do you wrong."

"Bet. Don't let the look fool you." He held his hands open wide so that Devon could get a good view of what he was talking about.

Although dressed in the latest gear, Rico had matured a bit with his choice of clothes. His black T-shirt was draped by a crisp blue blazer and a long diamond platinum chain. With jeans and a jazzy pair of shoes, he looked like he was getting plenty of money.

Before long, Devon and Rico had rapped for over an hour. They reminisced about the outrageous money making days of the past, and how Devon planned to be his number one seller once again. Devon boasted on his ability to take over blocks, and persuade customers to be loyal to him in the blink of an eye. Rico laughed quite a bit, and actually enjoyed Devon's prison stories.

Before ending, Rico asked one last time, "I got your

word, right?"

Devon extended his hand without hesitation or speaking. The two men locked eyes and confirmed their agreement with a rigid handshake. Rico's expression showed complete confidence, but his thoughts weren't as certain. *Everything might look good on the surface, but I gotta keep my good eye on this nigga.*

Chapter

6

When Carlie Stewart rose confidently to object, she felt the many pairs of eyes locked on her. Beside her, Marcus Dupree gazed smugly at the judge, while his mother and father watched nervously behind the defense table. The buzz was out, the state wanted life. Therefore, the pressure was on Carlie to produce.

For days, the headlines read, 'Double Murder', 'When Domestic Violence Goes Too Far', and 'Boyfriend Shoots Mother and Unborn Baby'. The court room was packed with family members of both the defense and the victim. The tense environment had everyone on edge, including the judge.

Carlie worked day and night to prepare for the day long trial, but nothing seemed to be going as planned. Even though Raymond Williard, the State's Attorney was questioning Marcus about shooting, he started getting into his personal life, making him angry, and confusing him altogether.

"Have you ever gone with a woman to get an abortion?" Williard asked?

Marcus looked puzzled. "Ahhhhh…"

"Have you ever paid for one?"

Marcus' eye's lit up. He had no idea where this was going. Before he could speak, Williard hit him with another difficult question. "Do you believe in abortion?"

"Why is his opinion on abortion important?" Carlie asked, in a fiery tone. "The question invades the witness' privacy Your Honor, and has nothing to do with the case."

"It does have something to do with the case!" shouted Williard. "If he were a God fearing man, he wouldn't have shot and killed his girlfriend and unborn child, Miss Saundra Kelly!"

Chatter began to fill the courtroom. Carlie knew the emotional damage the jurors would suffer from that comment.

"Objection!" she shouted. "Allegedly, sir." She shot Williard an evil look.

"Sustained," Judge Simpson stated, before banging his gravel.

Williard smiled. The jurors were already gazing at Marcus' arrogant expression. Instead of showing remorse as Carlie had instructed, he purposely sat with his hands folded, as if he were in charge of a board meeting. Marcus raised his chin even higher as Williard walked over to him.

"You killed her didn't you?" he asked abruptly.

"The hell I didn't!" Marcus shouted.

"Objection, objection, objection," Carlie yelled.

Marcus rose from his seat, shouted at Williard and shot nasty looks at the prosecution. None of this is what Carlie had planned. Over the past month, she had trained Marcus on how to handle the interrogation. She knew Willard would go for the guts and try to cause major outbursts in his favor. She had repeated the same questions over and over again in preparation for an event like this. Marcus was already seeing a therapist, and Carlie knew he could lie with a straight face, but truly believed that he was innocent.

The media had pumped so much bad publicity into the case that, at times, Carlie felt as if she didn't have a chance. Willard hated her like a long time enemy, and didn't have a problem showing it. He felt that Carlie was too new to the game, and had been handed her credibility on a silver platter without putting in any hard work. He was in line to be the next big shot of the city, but Ricky's influence with all the right people, was putting Carlie in some connected situations.

Carlie had no choice but to stand tall and handle any unexpected blows he sent her way. But from the looks of things, it wouldn't be easy. She thought about the latest alarm that added salt to the wound. She recently found out that the victim, Saundra Kelly was the *Chief of Police's niece*. Between that new information, and Willard's hate for her, her back was up against the wall.

As Carlie looked up, her interest in the case came to a halt. She had feared a surprise witness from the prosecution, but never this. Her voice was now monotone and low as she asked for a recess. Her face changed colors as if the wind had been taken out of her. *Could it really be him?* she thought.

"Are you sure you want a recess now?" the judge asked, puzzled by the request.

"If you would be so kind, Your Honor." Carlie's eyes

begged for his consent. There was no way she could execute her plan at a time like this.

Instantly, she glanced back over her shoulder. She closed her eyes and opened them again, just to be sure. Although his facial appearance remained the same, his eye-catching weight loss gave him the appearance of being slightly taller than before. Besides, his closely shaved haircut was really throwing her off. She was accustomed to a more thuggish appearance.

"Okay, then I guess I'll see everyone after lunch," Judge Simpson announced.

Carlie swallowed hard as she tried to catch her breath. As key people involved in the case quickly exited the courtroom, she took her time gathering her things. All sorts of ideas bounced back and forth around her mind. *How did he find me? Why is he here? And most importantly, how did he get out?* Small beads of sweat formed across her forehead. *Escape,* immediately came to her mind.

Careful about who would see her talking to Devon, Carlie waited for the last person to clear the room before speaking. Nervously, she kept her distance until there was no one left, but the two of them.

I'll just turn around and ignore him? Avoid him like the plague, she thought. "No, let's end this now," she mumbled to herself. "How did you get out?" she blurted out tensely.

"Is that how you greet the man who loves you?" Devon shot her his million-dollar smile.

Carlie felt his voice in the pit of her stomach. She couldn't believe old feelings were still there. His smile eased her fears just a bit, but didn't explain how he got out, or the reason for his visit.

"Why are you here, Devon?" She placed her hands on her

hips, trying not to stare.

His prison built body was nothing short of rock-hard muscle made for the strip club, and would cause any woman to stare. She thought about how she fell in love with him when he resembled an oversized sloppy wrestler. Now, as he stood before her with a better body, clean-cut look, and an even sexier smile, she knew walking away would be difficult.

"I came for you," Devon said.

"What do you mean?"

Carlie took a quick look toward the door, hoping no one would come in and see her with a fugitive. She fidgeted. "I mean just what I said. I came for you," he repeated. "I've been out for about two weeks."

"I'll ask you one last time. How did you get out?" She emphasized the *how*.

"On a technicality."

"What kind of technicality? Don't feed me bull-shit, Devon. Remember, I'm a lawyer."

Devon took two assertive steps forward. Carlie winced. "What are you doing?" she asked, in an uneasy tone.

Devon raised his brow as he opened his arms wide. "Let's start with a hug and then I'll tell you all about it." He laughed like a crooked politician.

Carlie stood still and looked him over like he was a complete stranger. She studied his trim waistline, and couldn't believe he'd gotten his body so polished. Still, in all, he was proving that his thug-like demeanor hadn't changed.

"So, you just gon' leave a brotha hangin'?" Devon moved full speed ahead, without giving Carlie a chance to flee. "I miss you," he said, holding her tight.

Carlie said nothing and firmly kept her hands at her side.

Devon's warmth felt good. *Real good.*

"Whether you know it or not, you need me," Devon whispered in her ear.

Carlie's insides moistened. The sound of Devon's voice, and the feel of his hardness pressed up against her brought back too many good memories. She thought about the fact that she hadn't had a great orgasm in years. *Don't be stupid — don't be stupid,* she kept telling herself.

Carlie came to her senses and forcefully backed away. She wondered why she had allowed herself to remain in Devon's hold for so long? What if someone saw her?

"We belong together, Carlie," he said, in a matter-of-fact tone.

For Carlie, this was beginning to resemble a scene from *Sleeping With The Enemy.* "I'm taken," she said, hoping this would end their conversation.

He laughed. "By who? Kirk?"

"Yes," she said softly. She hoped this wouldn't offend Devon and send him into some ballistic state.

After all, Kirk used to be his boy years ago. Not only did Kirk steal his girl, he betrayed him as well. In the street game, that meant payback would be a bitch.

Under normal circumstances, Carlie would be done too. Her actions were just as cruddy as Kirk's, but Devon had a soft spot in his heart for her. He'd hurt Carlie in so many ways prior to going to jail, that he cut her some slack.

"It's just a matter of time for him," Devon finally spoke.

"Is that a threat?"

Devon gave up the grittiest look possible. "It's a promise. That nigga betrayed me in many ways, so he's due. So, is he laying up at your crib?" He grinned wickedly. "Cause that nigga ain't got no real paper."

Carlie paused. Her heart beat like a loud drum. "How would you know?"

"I know everything. You find out more shit in jail than you do on the streets. So, you wanna tell me where he is?"

"No," she shot back.

"Umm, what if I said, I already know?" He smiled.

Carlie instantly thought back to the days when Devon would have her followed. She wasn't about to go back to feeling like a prisoner again. She was pissed off at Kirk, but not enough to allow Devon to hurt him. *Had Devon really been following them?* Scared for Kirk's life, she had to get to the bottom of things.

"I'll ask you one last time. How did you get out so early? You had the rest of your life to do?" she asked sarcastically.

Devon frowned. "I told you on a technicality. You don't believe me? Better yet, are you upset that I'm out?" His mood changed for the worse. "I guess your lil' degree got you all high and mighty. I'm the same nigga who supported you through school. You didn't ask so many questions back then!"

"I didn't know any better."

"Oh, you knew. You knew when you drove around town in fly cars. You knew better when you had your hands out for cash."

"Don't change the subject, Devon. I don't want to be seen with an escapee."

"You're so proper now," he joked. How 'bout dinner with an escapee?" He mocked her choice of words. "I'll allow your pussy-ass boyfriend to live a few more days, and I'll give you all the details about my release. I assure you, I'm legit."

"If I agree, will you leave now?"

"Oh, you don't want nobody to see us together, huh?"

"Devon, please…I'm working."

"Meet me tomorrow at seven."

"Where?"

"I'll pick you up in the front of your office."

Shocked, Carlie asked, "You've been to my office before?" She sighed. "Never mind, don't answer that. I'll meet you at Clyde's on Fifth Street. I'm sure you'll find it. Now, can you please go?"

As soon as the double doors shut, Carlie flipped open her laptop and went to work. She set up shop as if the courtroom were her office. With her cell phone in hand, and a notepad plopped on the table, the first call was to Jewell. She instructed her to call in a few favors and find out what she could about Devon being released.

After she ended her call with Jewell, she scribbled on her legal pad the names of several islands – Turks and Caicos, Cayman Islands, Cabo San Lucas, and Jamaica. She had to get away for a couple of days. She grabbed her cell phone in a hurry.

Her fingers worked overtime as she dialed Kirk's number. Calling him wasn't a part of her plan. She had hoped to play hard to get for as long as she could, but Devon put a stop to that. This was an emergency.

When Kirk answered, it almost crushed her pride to say something. "Kirk," she spoke loudly into the phone.

"Yeah, it's me," he answered.

"I think we should talk."

Kirk tried not to show how happy he was that she'd called. He figured she was done with him.

"No doubt, that's what I was thinking."

"I'm making reservations for us to go away in the morning. With the case and all, I can't concentrate here in town."

Kirk paused for a slight moment. "Tomorrow morning?"

"Exactly," she snapped.

"Can't you be disbarred for some shit like that?"

"No stupid. I'm ahead of the game. I'll call the judge to get an extension. I have a good reason made up already."

"Well, I'm picking up a car in New York," he said, sounding like he had another excuse on the tip of his tongue.

"Kirk, trust me when I say it would be in your best interest to leave the bitch and come with me!"

"Carlie, I'm not with anybody."

"Whatever. I'll call you back with the details." Click.

Chapter

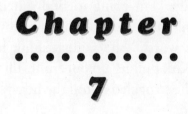

7

As usual, curbside check-in was packed. "Right here!" a bony, bigheaded skycap yelled. He stared Carlie down from top to bottom, and motioned for her to skip several spaces in line. Ignoring the pervert, she opted to head inside just as her cell phone rung.

"Your loss!" the skycap shouted, taking offense to the rejection.

"Hello," she answered, strutting inside the airport.

Wasting no time, her father yelled at the top of his lungs, "I can't believe some jack-leg judge would allow something like that to happen! A fucking technicality?" he screamed.

"Yes, calm down. Apparently the agent in charge and the prosecutor agreed in a written plea agreement, along with Devon, not to ask the judge to impose any more than twenty years." Carlie stopped momentarily in front of the American Airlines ticket counter to search for Kirk. "We both know that they intentionally wanted the judge to ask for more time. Obviously, Devon's latest lawyer was able to uncover all of this."

"What about the real crime here? He committed a crime! Not one, two or three, he's a regular at the jail house." Ricky breathed heavily. "I'm going to find out more. Carlie, stay away from him! You've got too much to lose."

"Oh, don't worry," she said, rushing her father off the phone. "I see Kirk pulling up out front. I'll call you when we get back." Carlie struggled to roll the heavy, black bag toward the outside door.

"Carlie, just what is your plan?" Ricky asked bluntly.

She was so accustomed to her father making this comment that she didn't know which situation he was talking about.

"What do you mean?" she questioned.

"When are you two getting married?"

"Married?"

"Yes, married. That's what two people do when they're in a serious relationship and living together."

"News break, Dad. We don't live together anymore!"

"Carlie, what are you doing? First you come up with a bogus story as to why I've got to take over your case while you're gone. The most important case of the year, I might add. And now you're leaving the country with someone that just moved out, or you put out!"

"Bye, Daddy," she hummed, in a soft-like tone. "Thanks for looking out."

As Carlie made her way back outside the doors, the morning rush was evident. Taxicabs moved in and out, dropping off families one after another. Kirk waved his hand, signaling Carlie to head his way, as he quickly copped a space near the end of the line, waiting to check their luggage. The single file line was filled with folks, both old and young, headed to the Caribbean with tons of luggage scattered about.

"Let's check in inside," she said. "It's cold out here."

"Honey, this is the best place to do it," an old country woman standing in front of Kirk interjected. "By the time you drag all of that stuff in there and wait in that zoo, you'll wish you'd stayed out here."

Carlie laughed at how the eighty-something year old woman had just invited herself into their conversation. She smiled, thinking about how she reminded her of her late Grandma Jean.

"You headed to Ochos Rios?" Carlie asked the woman.

"Not me, baby. That's for dead-beats. I'm going to Negril, Jamaica. Smoke me some weed, and chill. Ooh…Chile, I can smell it now."

Kirk and Carlie both laughed, until Carlie caught herself. She didn't want to give Kirk the impression that everything was okay. In fact, everything was wrong, but the time away was necessary.

As the cars pulled up, more and more passengers assembled in line. Before long, the line had stretched back three to four yards, and the counter became so crowded that the sky-caps began to walk out to the customers and toss their luggage into the appropriate places, based on destination.

"I told you we should've gone inside," Carlie whispered.

"Hand me your bag. We're getting close," he said.

Just as Kirk turned to grab Carlie's bag, he noticed China wearing a toboggan at the end of the line, conversing with a slender white woman. Covering his mouth, he panicked and thought about what to do. He watched closely, just to be sure his eyes weren't deceiving him. He wondered how long she'd been standing there.

"Yeah, I'm headed to Ochos Rios," China bragged. "What 'bout you?" she asked the woman.

"We're going to Negril," the woman replied.

China shot Kirk an evil grin from afar. Her foot was pointed outward and her arms crossed, signaling that shit was about to hit the fan. *Enough watching*, she thought. China marched out of line as if she had an adrenaline surge. Two forceful steps later, she was face-to-face with Kirk, and a respectful distance from Carlie. Her face boiled with anger.

"What she got that I don't got ? Huh, I need to know!" China pointed at Carlie, without looking at her directly. "Answer me, Kirk. You told me last night that it was over between the two of you!"

Kirk wasn't about to mess up the second chance he'd been given. "China, go home. You're lying. You don't belong here!"

"Oh, I'm lying? Who sucked on this all last night! Did I give myself a passion mark?" Her head bobbed back and forth as she whipped out her C cup right in front of the crowd. By now, all eyes were glued to the scene and the pur-ple-toned mark covering China's breast.

Carlie stood gracefully with a stiff expression. Her calm manner told the bystanders that she was the better of the two. She cut her eyes at China, checking out her cheaply worn clothes and fake Louis Vuitton bag. *Umh...I can't believe this shit*, she thought.

Carlie struggled for self-control as she thought about grabbing China by the neck and ripping her extra long, fake eyelashes from her brow. She couldn't believe any woman would have the nerve to show up in cheap, drugstore bought make-up, causing a big commotion. She wondered what the people around would think of her if she hauled off and hit China. Her thoughts shifted to what her father would think. Or what if she appeared on the news?

Carlie had never been the type to fight. Carlie normally liked to handle things differently. Although she was the daughter of a man who was once a hired killer, she was brought up to be mild-mannered and reserved like her late mother. Even in her younger days, when she hung with her backstabbing friend Zarria, taking off her earrings to scrap wasn't an option, but this kind of shit had pushed her to the limit.

Instantly, Carlie's thoughts got sidetracked by the skycap grabbing the woman's bags in front of her. "Where to?" he asked, carelessly throwing her bags to his left.

China's face grew serious again. While she uttered a series of profanities, spectators whispered under their breath. "So, you fuck me one night and her the next?" China stopped for a moment to study Carlie's natural beauty. Freshly arched eyebrows, long hair and hour-glass figure, all added to China's envy. "Fuckin' home-wrecker!" she yelled, and pointed in Carlie's direction. As her eyes began to water, she screamed, "Fuckin' puta, puta, puta, " as loud as she could.

As the old woman prepared to leave the counter, she whispered to Carlie, "Honey, you need to slap the shit outta that helfa. A young trifling bitch took my husband over twenty-four years ago. I regret not kicking her ass."

Carlie shot the woman a fake smile, pretending to be okay. Something in her knew China was telling the truth. Her deranged scowl said it all. As more people started to linger, the embarrassment became unbearable.

"Kirk, you're busted," she said with confidence. "How would she know you were coming here?" Carlie's tone remained unnaturally calm.

"Tell her, Kirk!" China screamed like an unruly brat and not a twenty-two-year old woman. "I followed his ass. He left my house this mornin' after eatin' pussy all night."

As China continued to rant, the skycap asked Kirk for ID to print their boarding passes, as if nothing was going on. He was strictly about making his tips. For a moment, Carlie stood saying nothing. She felt like a fool. She knew China wasn't lying, Kirk was definitely a down-town kind of guy. For Carlie, it was necessary to go down, right between the clit. He couldn't excite her any other way.

As soon as Carlie was handed their boarding passes, she decided to walk away and save her dignity. Kirk quickly followed behind her. Others in line wanted her to beat China down to the ground. Leaving her luggage behind, she could hear China's voice continue to soar.

"Hey, where y'all headed!" the skycap yelled. Carlie nor Kirk answered him.

"Send their shit to Negril," China answered the skycap, with a straight face and in a sexy-like voice.

"You bet," he said, as she slipped him a twenty-spot. *Hell, maybe I need to pull a few more scandalous switches to get some good tips*, he thought.

She winked at her little trick and followed several yards behind Kirk and Carlie. China rambled on as she followed them all the way to the line that had formed at the security gate. She revealed out loud as much as she could along the way about her relationship with Kirk. Bystanders stared at the animated scene causing them to whisper to one another throughout the airport. China ended with a bang, calling Kirk a fucking faggot right before being stopped at the security gate.

"No boarding pass, you don't come in," the guard said to China. He had seen what was going on, and was ready to have her escorted from the airport if she didn't leave peacefully.

Carlie knew everything she said was true, but wasn't going to give China the satisfaction of ruining the trip. She handed the guard her boarding pass, and gave China a foul look before heading through the checkpoint. Little did China know, the trip was all about saving Kirk from Devon.

* * *

At last, after the three-hour flight and the long ride to the hotel, the taxicab pulled up in front of the luxurious Togi Oceanfront Hotel.

"Checking in?" the handsome porter asked, in his strong Jamaican accent.

Just as he opened the door gracefully for Carlie, her mind immediately went to the movie, *How Stella Got Her Grove Back*. Lord knows she needed a buffed man, with some excitement. If she had the balls to cheat he'd be the one, for real.

She hesitated and took in the beautiful scenery before answering, "Yes."

"Shall I grab your luggage?" Every crystal white tooth in his mouth glistened.

"We have none," she answered, with a slight attitude. "No offense to you," she said. "I just seem to be having a bad day. Our luggage never made it to the airport. This way to check-in?" she asked.

Kirk shot the porter an evil look, and followed behind Carlie like the woman in the relationship. During the entire plane ride, he had considered offering some sort of apology or explanation, but there weren't any words to get him off the hook. Between coming up with excuses and scheming on how to get the money he needed from Carlie, he spent his time mulling over the situation and never said a word.

Approaching the counter, they were greeted by a woman with a wide smile. The tall, slender woman wearing a badge that read, *Wynetta*, spoke in a loud and friendly tone,

"Welcome to the Togi Hotel. How can I help you?"

Carlie handed the woman her Platinum American Express and drivers license. "Here's the confirmation number," she said, passing the woman a slip of paper with the detailed information. Carlie could always count on Jewell to have everything in perfect order when she traveled. "Is that all you need?" she asked.

"Yes, Ma'am. I must tell you that we have a note under your reservation." Wynetta hesitated to read the note clearly before speaking. "A representative called from American Airlines. Your luggage has been found. It was sent to Negril and will be arriving here tomorrow." She continued typing into the computer like that was final.

"Tomorrow?" Carlie fumed while Kirk said nothing. Again, this was all his fault.

"Yes. I'm sure we have plenty in our shops to accommodate you until then." Wynetta grinned. "I'm sure swim attire will be fine for the evening." Wynetta continued to punch information into the computer like a data processor. "How about I send some chocolate-covered strawberries and a bottle of our house champagne to the room?"

Carlie shot Kirk a, *don't even fucking try it look.* "That won't be necessary," she said, with a half-ass smile.

"Uh-uhh." Wynetta paused with a strange expression on her face. "Your card was denied."

Carlie's hands instantly covered her face. It took a few moments to gather her thoughts. *Why was all of this happening to her?* The feel of Kirk's heavy hand on her shoulder snapped her back to reality.

"Okay, try this one," she said, handing her Mastercard over.

Within minutes, Wynetta's same perplexed expression appeared. "Denied." Wynetta looked Carlie in the eye. "Why don't I get them on the line for you? Maybe there is some mistake."

"Good idea." As Wynetta dialed, Carlie went on to explain how last week, the credit card company called to say that someone had been charging clothes and all sorts of items to her credit card. They also said that it would be taken care of, investigated, and the card was good for use. Instantly, Carlie thought, *China!* She remembered Jewell saying that the items were shipped to a New York address. *Could this be another China scheme?* At this point, furious wasn't enough to describe her disposition.

Wynetta handed Carlie the phone. Before long, the representative had explained to Carlie that she had called in to cancel the card earlier that morning. Carlie refrained from explaining, realizing who had made the phone call.

"This bitch is starting to be a thorn in my side," she mumbled to herself. "Okay," she said, dismissing the thought of resolving the issue. "Thanks for your help." Carlie hung up, took the defeat like a pro, and handed Wynetta cash for the room. "Send me a bottle of hard liquor to my room, please," she said, grabbing the room key.

Hours later, Carlie woke up from her nap with Kirk staring into her face. "Are you sure you wouldn't be a little more comfortable over here on the bed with me?" he asked.

"No way," she snapped, lifting her head from the couch. Night had fallen and the room was nice and dim, just the way Carlie liked it. "I'd rather relax."

"I just wanna to talk," he replied, after seeing Carlie roll her eyes.

Even though she had calmed down tremendously since earlier, it was still difficult not to appear standoffish. After all, she had bent over backwards for Kirk over the past few years. She'd pretty much given up the single life for someone who wasn't really ringing her bells. Kirk's curly hair, and smashing smile just wasn't cutting it anymore, she wanted to be swept off her feet. Carlie couldn't help but to think about how much money she dropped on their spur-of-the-moment trip. When it was all said and done, $6,200 was the current tab.

The thought of her spending that kind of money on a man had her mind playing tricks. With Devon, she never spent a dime. From fine cars, jewelry and clothes, down to basic necessities in life, it was all on him. Carlie grinned, *he really knows how to spoil a woman.* She thought even further about Devon, and remembered how he had beat her time and time again in the past.

She realized that it wasn't Kirk's character to stoop to that level, but instead, he was now putting her through mental abuse. Being caught in a love triangle of scandal with Kirk and China, wasn't her idea of living. He was becoming more of a charity case. As far as she was concerned, China could have him. At this point, the only reason she was there with Kirk, was because he saved her from Devon in the past, and now what better way to repay him, than keeping him from harm's way.

"Carlie, let me explain."

Before she could shoo Kirk away, he was already firmly planted by her feet, licking her luscious toes. For Carlie, this wasn't a turn-on. Without delay, she jerked her foot away from his grip.

"Is that something you learned from China, 'cause you've never done that before?"

Kirk didn't answer because Carlie was right on point. "Listen, I wanna get things right with us. You know, set the record straight." He beamed inside, just at the sign of Carlie listening attentively. "You know, you're not perfect either. I caught you having a wet dream about Devon less than a week ago!"

"Nada," she said with sarcasm.

"Face it. You were caught red-handed. I'm willing to over-look that. All I want is for us to be together. That's why I'm selling these damn cars, tryna do the right thing. I know I need a real career, making some real money to take care of you." Kirk jumped at the chance to grab his vanilla folder containing the car dealership paperwork. "You see, if I can get this loan, I can make things happen."

Carlie briefly looked at the paperwork sprawled out across the table, as if she wasn't really interested. She had seen the same paperwork two times before. "$200,000?" she asked with a smirk. "What is the money being used for?"

"The start-up cost mostly." Kirk opened his hands wide, as if in thought. "The rent, cars, utilities, etc."

"How much have you made on the cars you've sold so far?"

Kirk thought quick. "Umh…maybe $25,000." He lied with a straight-face. But he knew given the chance, he could really make the car business work. Then he could stop pretending to sell cars.

"How come I haven't seen a dime of that money? You live, eat, shit and sleep at my spot."

"I promise, I'll start helping out. I just assumed you didn't want any help. You definitely don't need it."

"You don't have to help out, because when we get back, you're officially moving out!"

That comment cut right through Kirk's skin. He was living lovely at her expense. "C'mon, Carlie. Give me another chance."

"I'll tell you what. I'll sign for the loan, but the building goes in my name too. But this, by no means, says we're back together. We've got a lot of work to do. Let's take it day by day. For starters, get rid of China." Carlie thought about telling Kirk about Devon's talk of getting him back, but didn't want to rain on his parade. At least he's trying to get his life together.

Kirk pounced on Carlie like he'd won the lottery, and immediately popped the buttons on her shirt. Instead of resisting, she sat still while he dove in and sucked her perky, succulent breast. She breathed in pity, just glad to see him happy. His heavy breathing produced a much louder sound than hers, and helped him to get in the mood. Carlie exhaled once again as she felt the budge in his pants harden. Sex with

Kirk was like getting a pap smear – you never looked forward to it.

Like clockwork, she spread her legs, knowing where his tongue would land next. In the four years that they'd been together, Kirk couldn't seem to give her an orgasm unless it was with his tongue. At first it was a serious issue after coming off of Devon's loving, but now he does what he has to do with his mouth to please her, then goes inside for his. It was far more gratifying than having his dick flap around her clit aimlessly for hours, trying to create some foreplay.

Carlie winced after feeling Kirk's palm press her forehead firmly on the base of the couch, as he kissed her passionately in the mouth. "You smell so good, baby," he moaned. The aroma from the apple body lotion made him even hornier.

Carlie's eyes were closed when he surprised her and dumped the tray of succulent strawberries all over her belly. It was as if his tongue had developed a mind of its own, jumping from her erect nipples down to her sweaty navel. He alternated between biting into the strawberries and licking his woman with the juices.

While he continued to play tricks with his tongue, Kirk thought about giving Carlie a car wash, something he'd learned from China and treated her to on numerous occasions, but he couldn't fathom disrespecting Carlie in that way. She was too reserved and he had too much respect for her. The thought of holding her butt cheeks hostage and holding her up high in the air may have been okay, but sliding her entire vagina through his tongue wash may have been overboard.

The decision to head down-south was already made, but he prayed the extra touch would excite her. Planning to lick between her legs like a lollipop, he grabbed hold of her legs tightly and yanked her his way. The moment Carlie caught a glimpse of his dick up close and personal, a nauseous feeling invaded her stomach. *It's not little,* she thought, *he just doesn't know what to do with it.* She couldn't bear to fuck him at the moment. It had been a stressful day. She thought about how his pumps were slow and uneventful, and decided the orgasm wasn't worth it.

The moment Kirk began to struggle with her tightly fitted Capri pants, she knew it was time to make her move. He was ready to go to work.

"Oh…uhh…stop!" she yelled. Her hand pressed toward his face. "I hate to do this, but I seem to be itching."

"What?" Kirk's neck stretched.

"It might be a yeast infection."

"Oh…men don't get those," he said, pushing himself closer once again.

"Nooooooo. Let me…"

"Let you what? Whatever you got, I want!"

Carlie jumped up at the sound of phone ringing. It was her savior. She jetted across the room, tripping over Kirk's pants located in the middle of the floor. She prayed it would be the airline saying the luggage came early.

"Hello."

Carlie frowned into the phone. *This can't be for real,* she thought, as China shouted one obscenity after the next.

"I see you think this is a game!" she shouted. "I bet when this knife rips into your high and mighty ass you'll understand. You must not know, Dominican women will fuck you up!"

Carlie thought deeply for a moment. *Now, we've gone to*

physical threats, she thought in a frantic. She opened the curtains slightly like a suspect hiding out. *What am I thinking, she's not here.* Paranoid, she just listened to the screeching sounds, realizing that China wasn't going to give up. She looked over at Kirk and shot him a, *don't even think about getting none of this look.*

"The next time I see you, it's nightie night, puta!" China's voice level deepened. "That's what happens to hookers!"

Carlie opened her mouth to speak. Click! "Fuck it," she uttered, just after hanging up. "I'm too old for this shit!" she said out loud.

Chapter

8

Devon sat in his newly acquired 1988 Mustang, waiting to pay up. The discreet ride had been chosen as a neighborhood decoy, fitting in amongst the rest of the cars. Dressed in green army fatigues and dirty Timberland boots, he waited patiently, as if he were on a stake-out.

After only a few days in New York, Devon had already pleased Rico by making him more money than his average worker. As he counted each bill carefully, his mind made speedy future calculations. $50,000 was the month end goal. He could do it, Devon had always been a money making machine. The combination of good product, forceful leadership and fear, all helped to build his empire. Even though, he was moving and shaking, he clearly needed more go-getters on his team.

Smoothing over his workers had been his specialty. Way before Devon was locked down, he was a picture perfect CEO on the streets, and worked his runners like a sales force. Like major companies, Devon would give bonuses to those who performed the best. He searched for money hungry youngsters who liked to splurge their money regularly. Those who spent a lot would need to re-up from him faster, just to make enough money to keep shining. Increased profits, along with a cold ass whipping from time to time, kept his workers on top. No one could touch Devon.

Rico swiped his hand across the outside window, grasping Devon's attention. *This crazy-ass dude 'bout to get his head shot off,* he thought. Devon grabbed hold of his pistol, popped the lock, and Rico hopped in.

"You gotta lot of balls," he said.

"Why you say that?"

"You countin' money and shit out in the open. You askin' to get shot up," Rico smirked. "Besides, it's two o'clock in the morning. And nothin' goes down after two that's legit."

"A mufucka better come strong, 'cause I'm blastin' me a mufucka," he joked. "I'll take a leg, arm, or anything I can get. But if I get robbed, I'm definitely goin' home with some-thin' to show for it." Devon squeezed his .45 tightly before sliding it back beneath his leg. "This is for you," he said, handing Rico a stack of bills wrapped in a thick rubber band.

Without counting, Rico stuffed the bundle into his jack-et pocket. "How much?"

Devon let out a wild laugh. "There's a little extra in there for you. Seven thousand pays my bill for frontin' me the product, and five is just for being you. Besides, you a'ight for a short, pretty-boy Columbian mufucka." Devon laughed again.

"Yeah…only you can get away wit' a comment like that. That's 'cause you big, black, and look like you'll use up all of my man's bullets." He glanced back over to make sure his boys were still watching them closely. Rico expressed amusement with a slight snicker. "Be glad you know how to make me rich." He extended his hand for a quick shake. "In spite of everything, you a good dude."

"Oh, yeah," he nodded. "Remember that when I splatter your boy in the middle of the street. Why he ain't been comin' around lately?"

Rico hunched his shoulders. "He normally comes around only two or three times a month. He got Snake puttin' in his work."

"Yeah, that young boy look like he doin' a few things. Is he dependable?"

"So far." Rico shot Devon a strange look. "But in this game, how long does that last? Snake is happy as long as he keeps fresh gold in his mouth and money to party with."

They both laughed.

"Seriously," Devon said, abruptly stopping his laughter. "It don't seem like Kirk be out here long enough to keep good runners."

"You know he be shacked up with your girl up in Mass. most of the time." Rico checked Devon's expression to see if he was getting to him.

Devon twisted his eyebrows at the thought. His fist began to bang into one another harshly. "In life, loyalty means everything. He'll pay! I hope he got one of these," he said, lifting his shirt to show off his new bullet-proof vest.

Devon knew exactly where Kirk was. The private investigator he had following Carlie, reported that she and Kirk were in Jamaica until tomorrow. Devon tried not to think about the fact that Carlie never intended on keeping their lunch date. Luckily, he'd gotten word from the investigator the morning Carlie left and just headed back to New York.

"Get back at me," Rico said, exiting the car. "One of my ladies is waitin' on me." He grabbed hold of his dick, just as he always did when he thought of getting sexed.

"No doubt," Devon responded, pulling away from the curb.

Headed uptown, Devon had to make one more stop before going to his already furnished one bedroom. The lack of luxury in the efficiency wasn't important, considering he spent less than eight hours per day in the unit. It had been set up by the only people who had looked out for him since his release. Devon considered a switch, but wanted to live up to the lease obligation. All his life it meant nothing to tell a lie, but this time his word meant everything.

Pulling up to the convenience store on 149th Street, Devon glared out the window, searching for the Don King look-alike. He had only met him once, but remembered the way his grey hair stood fixed on top of his head. Seeing the big blue sign that read 24-hours, prompted Devon to go in for a snack while he waited. Parking across the street, he strutted like he owned the block. Between the bums on the street and the hookers on the corner, he appeared to be the only one around.

As soon as he entered the store, four eyes studied him carefully. "I ain't stealin' shit!" Devon shouted to the skeptical husband and wife team.

Their response was silent, but the wife was determined and kept a four yard distance, following Devon around the store. Pissed, he grabbed a pack of doughnuts and pretended to shove them down his pants. The panicked look on the Chinese woman's face excited him so much that he cracked open a pack of Oodles and Noodles and headed for the coffee pots.

"Let's give you somethin' to yell 'bout, bitch!"

"You buy!" she shouted.

"I will. I'm makin' my dinner," he shot back. Devon was enjoying making the woman angry. Her husband sat quietly behind the register, ready to pull his pistol at any time. Devon had no intention on killing tonight, he just wanted to see them sweat. "I hope your equipment can push through this," he laughed, showing off his bullet-proof vest.

"Take pack. Go now." The woman pointed to the front door.

Devon ignored her, and poured the contents of the pack into the boiling coffee pot filled with water. "Spicy chicken!" he shouted, in the woman's direction. He grinned with spite.

"That's an easy way to get sent back to the pen," the older gentleman said, walking into the store.

"I'm just havin' a little fun," Devon answered, in a more serious tone. "Besides, a brotha gotta eat. I ain't had shit all day." He licked his fingers, like he was at home cooking in his own kitchen.

"Let's head outside," the man said, nodding toward the door.

"I need a bowl," Devon joked.

"You buy. You buy!" the woman shouted.

Just as the yelling began, Devon spotted an officer outside the door. He grabbed a fork, the coffee pot, and headed toward the door. As he passed the counter, he threw a crisp one hundred dollar bill in the man's direction. "If it's more than that, bill me," he smirked. "This is good," he said, taking the first taste of his undercooked noodles.

No sooner than Devon got outside, his mood changed. The six-foot, forty-something year old man had his arms crossed, with each leg planted firmly in whip ass position. Unsure about what was about to take place, Devon sat his pot on the mailbox. He looked the man straight in the face.

"What's up?" he asked, hunching his shoulders.

"You making me look bad. That's what's up!" the man shouted. "Let's take a walk," he said, checking for nosey spectators.

Devon followed. He was down for a discreet spot, but rested his hand on his piece just in case. "This good," he said, stopping in front of an old building.

"You calling the shots?" the man asked.

"Look man, we both got business to take care of. You do you and let me do me."

"I wish you had said that when I gave you that ten thousand you needed. Or better yet, we coulda had your ass sleeping in the streets, instead of hooking you up with that nice efficiency." The old man smirked.

Devon thought about his apartment. It wasn't fancy, but it was safe. "Man, look, you gotta trust me."

"Huh, trust you. I don't even know you. You just some low-life drug- dealer that I got connected to for a moment."

"Look here, Don," Devon said, trying to provoke the man who obviously hadn't given up his real name.

"Yeah, you think it's funny. But I like you not knowing my name. It keeps my name out of the paper just in case I have to pop you one time." He grinned. "For now, buddy, you can just call me Don."

"If it's ass kissin' you lookin' for, I ain't yo man."

"No, but you'll be somebody else's man as soon as I send

your ass back to prison."

What...what...the fuck do you want from me!" Devon roared.

"What I want is for you to move a little faster. We're looking for a quicker return on our money, if you know what I mean." He winked. "I might have to show up on your strip if things don't pick up."

Devon fumed. "You playin' real dirty. Watch yourself."

"Or what?" Don challenged.

"You know what," Devon ended, walking away. *I ain't 'bout to catch a charge over some old ass nigga,* he thought.

Chapter

9

Carlie held her forehead pressed flatly on the desk. Exhausted, she was beginning to realize that her life wasn't as flamboyant as she planned. Yes, she was making loads of money, but was becoming a pill-popping junkie. Nightly, her routine had become swallowing 1000-milligrams of Tylenol, in an attempt to subside the skull-banging headaches. *China, Devon, and the Dupree case, were all driving her crazy.* It didn't help that since her return from Jamaica, she was nervous about having to sleep alone for the first time in years.

Carlie made it perfectly clear to Kirk that he had to move out, and that they would take things slowly. And it was mandatory for his deranged side-piece to be scratched from their equation. Kirk vowed that he wouldn't see China or any other woman again. He joked when he told Carlie that Beyonce could walk past him butt naked and he wouldn't even look. She laughed, but in a strange way believed that he might eventually change.

He told her he loved her every chance he got, and tried to

show her by spending money he didn't really have. He tried any and everything to convince her. Even though she claimed material things weren't important, he knew her from the old days, and couldn't imagine her not being materialistic.

Kirk showed how desperate he was to make her happy when he visited an unknown pawnshop a few blocks away from the diamond district. He walked right in and picked out a pair of cheap three-carat clustered diamond earrings. The price was right, the bling was right, but Carlie didn't seem too excited. She could spot cheap jewelry anywhere. She was used to Devon spoiling her with single solitaires and loose diamonds, expensive ones at that.

It irked Kirk to know that Devon would never have gotten Carlie any jewelry from a pawnshop, but he had to keep up somehow. Devon had given her just about every piece of jewelry sold. So, Kirk went for unusual pieces Carlie couldn't trace back to the pawnshop. He knew his woman liked the finer things in life, and even if it meant used jewelry that made him look like a baller, he'd do it. Besides, Carlie would never know. For some reason, Carlie decided to act as if she liked the earrings. She had faith that everything would work itself out.

At the thought of believing in Kirk, she raised her head with a gust of energy. She had promised to leave her personal business at home, away from the office. She couldn't believe that another woman could cause her to lose sleep and get deep under her skin. After the first four nights of sleeping only with her .380 Caliber, she was happy the weekend was finally approaching. Kirk was coming to stay for the weekend, which would allow her to sneak a little bit of rest.

She sat in her plush office chair, fumbling through the

many depositions, police reports and statements, spread about the desk. She took out a pen and yellow legal pad, ready to review the information for the tenth time.

To her left, lay Marcus Dupree's long rap sheet, including numerous arrests for domestic battery, illegal gun charges, theft, and several reckless driving violations. Carlie shook her head at the thought of Devon's rap sheet that rested under another pile of papers. Jewell had been instructed to pull all pertinent and updated records on Devon.

"Okay," she mumbled to herself. "I can't focus on Devon right now. My client needs all of my attention." Her pen moved carefully across the notes. "Neighbors told police they heard commotion coming from the apartment about 11 p.m. And Marcus admits he was causing a commotion outside the door around that same time. Uhm…" Carlie checked both sides of her chart.

One of Carlie's strengths through law school was to rationalize and set up plans of action. She had a deep sense of forecasting what could possibly happen down the road and figuring out options and the best way to deal with situations. Especially, when it came to criminal cases. Unfortunately for her, this skill didn't carry over into her personal life. She thought about Ricky's favorite saying, *what is your plan?* She sat up straight, trying her best to refocus.

Just then she realized Jewell was peeping around the door. *I thought I told her no interruptions.*

"Yes, Jewell," she said, in an unmannerly tone.

"I just thought you'd like a cup of coffee to help keep you up since you haven't been sleeping at night."

Carlie felt horrible. She was just about to order Jewell out until she realized how rude she'd been to her over the last few days. "Sit down a moment," she said, extending the invitation with a more welcoming grin. "I'm just having a rough moment.

"I know…"

"Tell me what you think about this. Marcus Dupree claims he went to visit his girlfriend the night of the murder to confront her about another guy. He admits being there, but says when he got there she was already dead. He called the police from her house." Carlie banged on the desk. "Is he that calculated and smart that he would call the police from her house, if he killed her?" Carlie raised her voice and looked closer into Jewell's face. She desperately needed someone to help her make sense of this case.

"Could be." Jewell shrugged her shoulders. "You never know what people are capable of. That's why I never judge a book by its cover."

Carlie looked deep into her normally hyper secretary's face. It was as if Jewell was directing the comment to her. Quickly, she overlooked her disapproving expression. "Okay, as I was saying…he called 911, saying that she had committed suicide and to send help right away. Would a murderer do that?"

Jewell shrugged her shoulders once again.

"And there was no weapon found at the scene!" Carlie flung her head down on the desk. Her frustration was evident. "I've got to win this case," she mumbled, with her face pressed into the desk. "I can't let an innocent man go to prison."

"How do you know he's really innocent?" Jewell whispered.

Carlie jerked her head upward. "What do you mean?"

"I mean you're so quick to put your trust in men."

Carlie shot her an awkward look. "Alright Jewell, we've had a nice chat. I'm done sulking."

"Okay," she said, jumping up from her seat. "But just think about what I said. I see what Kirk is taking you through. You don't deserve it." Just as Jewell turned to walk away, the phone rang.

"Don't bother, I'll get it," Carlie said, with a slight attitude. "Stewart and Associates, how may I help you?" At the sound of his voice she hung up.

Two seconds later it rang again. "Hello," Carlie answered harshly, before Jewell could answer. At this point, she knew her secretary already thought she was a fool. "What is it, Devon?" she asked.

"What happened to our lunch date?" He spoke calmly in a sexy-like tone.

Carlie was caught off guard. She was expecting a word battle. She knew how unruly Devon could get, especially since she had deliberately hung up on him. "I've been busy. This case I'm working on has me on pins and needles. I just couldn't make our meeting."

"The trip didn't do you any good?"

Carlie removed the phone from her ear and just looked at it. *How did he know that?* Instantly, she jumped out her seat and peeked out the corner window. Every man fitting Devon's description sent a nerve bolting through her body. She was becoming a paranoid fool.

"Everybody deserves a good trip once in a while. So, when are you free? I wanna catch up just a bit." Devon talked as if he was the perfect gentleman and had never laid a hand on Carlie a day in his life. "It seems like you need a shoulder to cry on, rely on, or rub on," he joked. "No, in all serious-ness, I know you're goin' through it at the moment. I owe you this."

"Where are you?"

"Wherever you want me to be." His voice lowered.

"No serious. I need to know." Carlie's demeanor was a bit frantic.

"I'm in New York. But if you need me, I'll be there asap." Devon's voice became extremely soft. "You know I mean it."

Whoa…had Devon changed? His look definitely did a 360 and now his personality — Devon so caring? Somebody is play-ing a trick on me.

"What about…"

"I tell you what, I'll come out your way on Saturday. This way, your mind isn't on work."

"Can't do it on Saturday," she quickly responded. Kirk would be at her house for the weekend.

"Why don't I come tonight?"

"Devon, stop it."

"No really. Your mouth says no, but your body says yes." Devon's tone changed. He seemed extremely serious about his plans. "I'll see you around ten tonight."

"Devon, don't show up at my house. I've got a gun."

"You would never think 'bout killin' me. Deep down inside you still love me, but it's okay. I still love you too."

Carlie scrambled for the paperwork identifying Devon's rap sheet. Murder, drug trafficking, conspiracy, intent to sell firearms to a minor…

Naw, she thought. *It would never work. I've got to get myself together, especially if I'm gonna make things work with Kirk.*

"I tell you what. Let's shoot for Monday at noon."

"No doubt. If that's all I can get, I'll take it. Don't stand me up this time."

"You just don't get it, do you?"

"Get what?" he asked nonchalantly.

"We haven't been together in years, and we're not gettin' back together. So I really don't see the point in this little reunion."

He hesitated and breathed deeply into the handset. "I'll see you Monday. Or, I just might come in town early and watch your beautiful face from afar." He laughed wildly. "Besides, Kirk will be six feet under by noon."

Carlie's expression changed. She knew Devon was probably serious. She ended the conversation and dialed Kirk's number. *No answer.*

* * *

Back in Harlem, Kirk stretched out his flabby body while China positioned him comfortably in the plush lounge chair. His head rested near the top of the chaise, while his legs dangled below.

The mood had been set. More than enough candles had been lit to start a three alarm fire. The scented candles complimented the exotic lavender and vanilla smell of the room. Rings of tea lights lined the tables in fitted holders flickering in the dim light. Before entering the house, Kirk contemplated the idea of China asking him to come over due to a fake emergency. He had promised himself that he had to make things right with Carlie. He needed money. To his surprise, as soon as he arrived, she yanked him inside and nibbled at his pants like a junkyard dog. He couldn't resist.

With a dreamy-eyed look, she placed the blindfold across his face, covering his eyes. Excited, he fantasized about what China had up her sleeve this week. Kirk, without a doubt, enjoyed the spontaneity of not being able to see.

Grabbing his crotch, she played with his balls, for a quick tease. Within seconds, he was on fire. China snatched his pants well below his knees. Sweat poured and his breathing grew rough as he waited anxiously to see what would be next.

China knelt down, searching for the right position. She quickly waved her hand across his blindfold to be sure his vision was completely blocked. She smiled at the thought of not getting a response from him. *Perfect, he can't see*, she thought.

China continued with her mission. She had searched long and hard for two weeks for the best injector. Her plan had to work. Cautiously, she unwrapped the two-inch thick turkey injector from the towel, just to make sure it was still there. After a quick check, she threw the towel and the injector close to her side, next to the spill-proof plastic container.

Carrying out the mission, China grabbed hold of Kirk's enlarged penis. She licked hungrily at the underside of his shaft for an instant tease. Kirk's heart thumped hard, nearly jumping from his chest. He let out a loud moan the moment China wrapped her lips around the ballooned head.

"Damn, girl!" he shouted.

China smiled at Kirk's outburst. *Got him*, she thought. She snatched Kirk's hand without removing her juicy lips, and guided it toward her breast to get him deeper into the mood. The need for him to cum in that position was important.

While Kirk squeezed each breast violently, China sucked harder and faster. With his head thrown back in ecstasy, Kirk squirmed, lifting his butt cheeks high in the air. *So close*, she thought. Her strokes intensified and her head moved up and down like a contestant bobbing for apples. Just as he was about to release, China struggled to use one arm to grab the necessary items. Within seconds, she had opened the lid on the plastic container ready for the explosion.

"Oh, shit…uh…uh…!" he hollered, sounding like he had a speech impediment.

Just as he squirted, China pressed her left arm against his chest, signaling him to continue laying back. Kirk was in such a pleasurable daze that he had no idea what was going on. Nor did he care; it felt so good. Secretly, China stroked his manhood filling the plastic container with several ounces of sperm. She had to think swiftly. Through her research, she knew the sperm wouldn't remain effective for long unless it was frozen. Instantly, she jetted to the bathroom, leaving Kirk sprawled out in a frenzy.

"Hey, where you goin'," he yelled out. "It's your turn."

"No thanks, the toilet is callin' me," she responded, holding her stomach.

"Damn, you sure know how to spoil the moment."

China shot him a fake smile and hurried to the bathroom. Inside, she shut and locked the door. Her body slid to the floor with her back firmly planted against the door, making sure Kirk couldn't enter. She breathed heavily as her hands shook when she whipped out the injector. She had done her homework and was careful to choose one with holes to evenly distribute Kirk's sperm inside of her. China read the capacity on the injector. *Four ounces*, she thought, *more than enough to get me good and pregnant.*

Within seconds she had used the plunger to pull enough potential babies into the turkey injector. Her head rested comfortably against the bathroom door while her mouth hung open.

"Just like a tampon," she said softly, trying to convince herself. China let out a silent sigh as she slid the injector inside. "Yes, I know that's it!"

She grabbed the cordless phone and dialed Carlie's cell number. She laughed crazily when she heard her voice. "Did Kirk tell you we're havin' a baby?" she bragged.

Carlie held the phone in a state of shock. She figured China was just trying everything. *Surely, she wasn't pregnant,* she thought.

"We'll invite you to the baby shower, bitch!" Hearing Kirk's footsteps prompted China to hang up. She gathered the items from the floor and tossed them underneath the sink. Opening the door, she jumped on Kirk like a maniac. "You wanna hear the good news?" She grinned with the most mischievous spirit he'd ever seen.

Chapter

10

Shortly after three in the morning, an old black pick-up sat discreetly at the tip of Greenwich Hills. The historic neighborhood was home to the wealthy, and the streets were filled with beautiful aged oaks. The normally quiet area appeared spooky, like a scene from a horror movie. As the wind blew slightly, the scar-faced man inside the car picked at his tooth with a straw and watched the targeted house closely. Shocked, the unidentified watchman sat up straight at the sight of a yellow cab pulling up slowly outside of Carlie's three-story home.

"Right here is fine," the mysterious woman said, in an anxious tone. The cabby had cruised the extremely quiet neighborhood for over thirty minutes, and was pleased to hear that the woman was getting out.

The cab driver shot her a funny look. "Which house is it?" he asked, trying to be a gentleman.

"I said here is fine!" the woman said.

A woman wearing dark shades, and no idea where she's

going at this hour — trouble, the cab driver thought to himself. Something wasn't right, but he didn't have time to stick around and figure it out. There was money to be made. "That'll be fifty-two even," he said.

Wearing a trench coat and *nothing* underneath, the woman in disguise exited the cab at the top of the street and searched for any sign of an address. Walking toward the streetlight, she decided to check the house that was slightly lit.

"Shit…1492." China quickly looked down at the paper, realizing that Carlie's address was 1483. Without delay, she darted across the street and scrambled back and forth until she located the house. Spotting the huge wooded doors and elegant outdoor furnishings, China's envy increased.

"This high and mighty bitch don't even have a gate," China smirked, thinking she had one up on Carlie.

She headed around back, creeping like a spy on a secret operation. Although she had made a duplicate key to Carlie's house months ago, she felt a bit uneasy about going in without first checking the perimeter of the house. She didn't want any surprises, like a huge Doberman jumping out to attack her. This had been planned for days, so she wanted everything to run smoothly without any glitches.

She smiled at the thought of how excited Kirk would be when she entered and dropped her coat. Her nakedness would surely have him hooked. And Carlie would know the truth when the two of them fucked right before her eyes. To others, China's plan would probably be viewed as psychotic, but to China it was picture perfect.

Just as she reached the back, China noticed a pair of curtains moving a little from the neighboring house. The shadow inside quickly darted to the left, and stood stiffly, not wanting to be noticed. But China didn't care. She was still going in.

After fumbling around for the key, she smiled as she inserted the key into the lock with ease. "He's mine now," she said, turning the knob. Inside, China crept around on her tippy-toes, as if she didn't have on five-inch, fuck me stiletto pumps. She spent the first two minutes on the main floor in the darkness, touching Carlie's expensive artwork and keepsakes. Her jealously tripled after seeing Carlie's fancy belongings.

A 52-inch custom flat screen T.V. hung from the wall, while three separate fireplaces outlined the room. China thought about taking a seat on the huge suede lounging chair, while she studied a photo of Carlie and Kirk. "So, the bitch think she's living good, huh," China huffed. Instantly, she threw the frame, aiming for the couch, but it landed on the Travertine tile.

Carlie jumped at the sound of the frame hitting the tile. "Kirk, wake up," she said with anxiety. "Did you hear that?" She shook his arm with force, trying to wake him.

"It's nothing. Go back to sleep," he mumbled groggily. Kirk knew Carlie had been a basket case lately and disregarded her nervousness.

Instantly, Carlie threw the covers back in a frenzy and reached for her gun underneath the mattress. She looked over at Kirk, expecting him to have her back, but he had returned into a deep sleep.

Maybe, I'm overreacting, she thought. Carlie considered getting back in the bed, until she thought she heard the steps creaking. Within seconds, she was out of her bedroom and headed down the steps. At the bottom of the staircase, she looked swiftly to her left, then her right like an episode of *Cops.*

Dashing into the living room, she wondered if Kirk would hear her if she screamed. With her .380 held firmly in front of her, both palms had built up plenty of sweat. Even though she had been to the shooting range many times in her younger years, holding the gun to save her life was totally different. Devon taught her to shoot at point blank range and drilled in her —*it's either them or you.*

Scared of getting killed, Carlie thought ahead about how much cash was in the house. Her mind worked overtime, like a human calculator. *Two thousand, two hundred should be enough to bribe anybody.* She thought about turning on the lights, but then it hit her. She knew her house like the back of her hand and the intruder didn't.

Carlie ran her hands along the walls, knowing exactly where she was going. As she crossed the foyer, a beam of light from the outside light post shone through. At the same time, a petite shadow appeared from behind. Carlie turned without hesitation to startle the intruder.

In the dimly lit shadows, China's face appeared. Her deep black eyebrows creased at the sight of the gun. Thoughts of her next move bounced around her mind like a ping-pong ball. *Would Carlie kill her?* Just as she thought about giving up, China saw Kirk walking up carefully behind Carlie. In a flash, she yanked her belt and dropped her coat to the floor.

At that moment, the sound of the firearm shocked them all. The impact of the hollow tip bullets knocked China off her feet. She was as helpless as a deer on a country road when the first bullet lunged through her chest.

"Ugh," she moaned, grabbing at her chest. Her eyes showed defeat as she collapsed on the floor. China's arm reached out to Kirk, who stood quietly with his jaws hung low.

Carlie still didn't realize Kirk was there. She thought about screaming for him to see if China was still breathing. But instead, she fired the second shot, aiming for her head like a seasoned killer.

Kirk yelled out, "China!" at the top of his lungs.

Carlie turned to him with a blank look on her face. Her body froze in an immediate state of shock. She wasn't sure whether to rejoice or feel remorse as she watched Kirk's stalker lay naked on the floor. When Kirk reached over to Carlie's shaking body to take hold of the gun, tears spilled from her face. With her stomach feeling like a bottomless pit, she thought for sure someone had thrown her off a cliff.

"Oh, my God!" she cried. "What did I do?" She pounded her head back and forth into Kirk's wide chest. His face reeked disapproval, but he reluctantly threw his arms across her for comfort. He tried to comfort Carlie and hurry to help China at the same time. As his body tried to move toward China's, Carlie intentionally kept Kirk from moving away from her. She sobbed on his shoulder, holding him back. "Oh, my God, Kirk!"

"Carlie, we gotta help her!" He took a deep breath, released Carlie, and rushed to China's side. Everything was happening so quickly. Before he knew it, the blood that seeped from the side of her head was all over his hands. He panicked as he noticed China lying stiff as a corpse in a casket. "China!" he called out. No response, no breathes, no movements.

"Kirk," Carlie called out, in a low voice.

He turned around swiftly. "She's dead! What happened?" he asked, in a strange tone.

"I don't know!" she cried out. Carlie's hands scrambled through her hair like a crazy woman, and her body shook like a crack addict. As her nose continued to run, she began to pace the floor. She spoke at the most rapid speed she'd ever spoken before. "I came downstairs! She was just standing there! Something was in her hand! I don't know, I don't know, it was something…"

"Calm down, Carlie."

"I can't," she shot back, glancing at China. "We gotta call the police."

"And say what? You shot a woman that I recently had dealings with?"

Carlie collected herself fast. She thought about all the scary comments she'd heard from her clients about being locked up. Instantly, she had visions of a butch-type woman dragging her out of bed in the middle of the night and paying the guard to look the other way while she got her womanhood taken. The entire scene was beginning to make her dizzy.

Carlie snapped from her erratic behavior as she heard the sirens approaching. She immediately thought about calling Ricky. Her heart said he would be able to figure out what to do. He was a mastermind at getting criminals off the hook, and she knew he'd always be there, whether she was locked up or not.

Kirk shot over to Carlie, grabbed her by the shoulders, and spoke directly into her face. "Listen to me and fast!" He patted her cheeks to make her focus. "The police will be here in a minute."

"I know, I know," she said sniffling. Carlie knew she had to get herself together.

"Say that you thought it was a robbery."

"I did," she said, giving Kirk a funny look.

"Ohhhh...okay," he responded with sarcasm. "When you came downstairs, you thought she had a gun," he said, rehearsing for the moment the police entered.

"Kirk!" Carlie shouted with anger. "I'm going to tell just what happened. I did think we were about to be robbed or even killed. When I fired, I was just protecting myself!"

"Even the second time?" he asked, with a skeptical expression.

Just then, a tall shadow appeared to be getting closer to the house. From the window, Kirk noticed the red and blue lights flashing, and several officers close to the front door.

Kirk yelled out, "We're okay, I'm opening the door!"

As soon as he opened the door, several officers had their guns drawn in ready-set position. "She lives here." He pointed to Carlie sitting on the bottom step in a flood of tears. "She doesn't," he said, pointing to where China lay in a pool of blood.

An officer rushed over to China and took her pulse. She looked to be in a deep sleep. "Has the ambulance been called already?"

"We didn't have a chance to," Carlie responded sadly. She gave the officer a puppy dog look.

Immediately he grabbed his walkie-talkie and dispatched an ambulance, even though he knew China was good and dead. "Your neighbor called to say an unknown person was trespassing out back over thirty minutes ago. The gentleman called back when he heard gunshots."

It was apparent that Carlie lived in a well-to-do neighborhood, because the ambulance arrived within five minutes. The hustle and bustle of the medics rushing in the house had Carlie worried to the tenth power. Her mind fast-forwarded to the skinny medic on the floor saying she's dead alright. Then she thought she was being hit with another hallucination when she heard the medic say severe head trauma. She blinked.

"What did he say?" she asked Kirk.

He ignored her and kept his eyes on China's body.

The medic stood as his co-worker rushed in with the oxygen and mask. "I believe she's in a coma!" he shouted, moving faster than before. The thought of her life possibly being saved increased everyone's speed. China was now believed to be unconscious, not dead.

The medical team worked quickly to get China out of the house and into the ambulance. They counted to three out loud in unison, as they lifted her body onto the gurney. As they whipped past Carlie, she nearly jumped out of her skin as China's hand made a jerky movement.

After China's body was out the door, over fifteen officers and detectives entered and scattered like roaches. The mood had changed from concern for China's well being, to a questioning session. Several officers took turns writing in their notepads, while sharing strange looks with one another.

Nearby, Kirk stood in a daze for nearly twenty minutes as the spot where China's body had laid was outlined in white chalk. The scene reminded him of a movie made for Hollywood. As people walked in and out, his feelings for China erupted. *Did she love him that much?* He couldn't believe that Carlie actually shot and possibly killed the woman who truly loved him.

Travis Peters, the senior detective on the scene watched every move Kirk made closely before speaking up. "Can I see you over here, sir?" he asked Kirk, moving toward Carlie.

He could sense Carlie's frustration and had already discovered she was a lawyer, and the daughter of the infamous, Ricky Stewart. He paced the floor in his normal retro attire and three-inch afro. The tie-dyed long shirt and numerous African chains didn't fit his persona as a no-nonsense detective, but the respect he received from his co-workers showed that he was the man.

He slapped hands and returned dap to every officer that passed. The scene was becoming more of a social event than a crime scene, until Travis started cracking the whip on his investigators. A veteran of the force for over thirty-five years, Travis was burnt-out. He'd uncovered all kinds of cases in his day, and never got the promotions he deserved. With one foot out the door, retirement was looking good. He just wanted one last case to make him an official legend.

Travis extended his hand toward Carlie. "Ms. Stewart, we're almost done here. Everyone will be leaving shortly. Why don't you go on up and get some sleep." His mannerism impressed Carlie. "You can come down to the station tomorrow to give your official statement."

Carlie hesitated until Kirk interjected. "I'll show them out. Go on up," he added. "You've had a rough night."

"Yeah, this nice young man will finish up down here." Travis took out a cigarette and looked Kirk over from head to toe. "So, you were so out of your mind that you couldn't call the police or ambulance either?"

Kirk immediately took offense. "I told you I came down after I heard the gunshots."

"Uhm…that's right. I forgot." Travis smirked. "And you knew this woman, right?"

"Right," Kirk answered with concern. In his mind, he'd already decided that if it came down to it, he wouldn't go to jail because of Carlie.

"Side-piece?" Travis smiled and nudged Kirk in the shoulder.

"We used to date. But that was over weeks ago." Kirk was close to shitting his pants. "Look, detective, I'm not sure what you're getting at. I didn't shoot that woman. She came here I guess to rob my girl."

"Yeah, I forgot. I guess she forgot to put some clothes on." Travis stuffed the old looking cigarette in his mouth, lit it and headed out the door. "Sleep easy for now, but if this turns into murder, there'll be problems."

Kirk stood dumbfounded, while his mind played tricks on him. *I'm not the suspect here. Hell, my fingerprints aren't on the gun. Carlie admitted to shooting her. Why am I on fucking trial?*

Twenty minutes later, Kirk shut the door behind the last officer. Fingerprints had been taken. All sorts of hair samples, pictures and yellow tape covered the three-story home. Kirk skipped several stairs, racing to look at Carlie face-to-face.

"Did you know it was China before you shot her?" he blurted out.

Carlie was stunned. "No," she responded curtly.

"You ain't being straight. But I'll tell you what, when we go down town tomorrow, I'll go along with your story as long as you go along with mine."

"What are you talking about?"

"I was standing there when you blasted China. You knew it was her." Kirk looked at Carlie with contempt. "She wasn't a threat. You wanted to shoot her!"

Carlie's eyes grew to the size of balloons. "That's not true," she sobbed.

"It's okay, baby. I'm here for you. Just know they might try to make it seem like she was shot because we were sleeping together."

Carlie looked up into Kirk's eyes as he grabbed her tightly. She wasn't sure where he was going with this.

"I just don't want to give the wrong impression. It's better to leave them believing that our relationship ended smoothly weeks ago. You feel me?"

"I guess."

"I just hope she lives. If she doesn't, that's a murder charge!"

"Not murder. Self-defense!"

"Yeah, self-defense." Kirk kissed her in the mouth.

To Carlie, it felt more like a persuasive kiss than a passionate one. For Kirk, he knew he had her in a vulnerable position and would be getting more than kisses in the near future.

Chapter
• • • • • • • • • •
11

"This is the real world, young soldier! You ain't in the joint no more!" the officer yelled, his knee jammed in Devon's back. "I gave you enough chances. It's time to put slime back in the can!"

"Man, what the fuck you sayin'?"

"It's always been clear as to what I'm saying. You just wanna do you. In case you haven't noticed, I'm the head nigga in charge!" Don yelled, moving closer to Devon's face.

As the clinking sound of the handcuffs caught Devon's attention, he looked back at the tall gentleman and wondered how he got the position of an informant caseworker. And why did he have to be assigned to him? He didn't fit the description at all. He was supposed to fit in so that no one suspected anything. Instead, he looked to be in his sixties and stood out like a sore thumb. *The Don King hair definitely had to go.*

"Look, man, what you want from me?" Devon asked.

"What you promised us," Don responded.

"I'm workin' on my part. How can I get enough evidence on Rico if I don't get into the game?" He glanced to his left, only to notice two unmarked cars pull up across the street. *Why in the hell was he calling back-up?*

"You seem to be enjoying this shit and making a good living in the process. We fronted you $10,000 to get started. You ain't gave us shit back, or no concrete evidence either."

"I wasn't supposed to pay that money back."

"You wasn't supposed to be getting rich either," he shot back, while tightening the cuffs. "I've sat and watched you sell drugs freely, carry weapons, and steal, amongst other shit. You walking the streets like you ain't in the snitch program!"

Devon looked back, while his eyes begged for mercy. "Can you pump your brakes and take these cuffs off? We seem to be bumpin' heads for no reason. I'm close... real close. For real," he said, in a convincing voice. "Plus, it's broad daylight. I'on need to be seen out here with you."

Don reached out, pretending to unlock the cuffs. Devon took the opportunity to glance at his gold-plated tarnished class ring. *Damn, 1956, this mufucka needs to be retired!*

"Gimme one reason why I should let you up?"

"Cause you need this case to work. It'll make you look good."

Devon's comment made good sense to the agent. He inserted and turned the key, while releasing Devon from his grip. "You playing with fire, young man. You think we don't know that you paid *our* investigator to go to Massachusetts to spy on your little girlfriend. That fool was spotted on her block by a neighbor the same night she shot somebody, and now he's under investigation. All because you acting like Tony Montana."

The rest of the agent's words were a blur to Devon. He stood glassy eyed at the thought of Carlie shooting someone. "Was she hurt?" he blurted out.

"Who?"

"Carlie?" Devon questioned, like Don should've known who he was talking about. He couldn't figure out why the investigator hadn't called him. *I paid that mufucka three thousand dollars and he ain't call me!* Devon fumed.

"This ain't about a woman," Don stated, pressing his middle finger in Devon's chest. "This is about you staying on the streets." He shook his head with disgust. "Two things. You don't run the streets, and for now, we run you. You better set Rico's ass up quick. We want concrete evidence. Come up with something on your own, or you'll be wearing a wire by next week."

Devon shook his head, no. "I ain't wearin' no wire," he said, in a delirious state.

"Then buy enough cocaine from Rico on the strip. We want photos. Our people are in place. Do your part!" Don checked over his shoulder suspiciously, and turned back to Devon. "You act like you don't know what time it is, player. All these pics of you two ugly motherfuckers ain't doing the case no good."

Devon frowned at the old man calling him ugly. He thought about saying fuck everything and just splitting his head down to the white meat before going back to prison. He wasn't willing to be a slave for nobody. He wanted the conversation to end so that he could call Carlie.

"In case you didn't notice, the original $10,000 you gave Rico was marked. When we bust him, we hope to find some of that marked money. And since you getting so much money nowadays, big gangsta." He nodded his head and turned his lip upward, clowning Devon. "You gotta start swapping whatever money you give Rico for our marked money." Don stopped to check his watch.

Devon had a puzzled look. "Somethin' don't smell right."

"It's not rocket science. You need to be giving him more marked money instead of the money you've been giving him on a regular." Don spoke to Devon as if he were a child, trying to learn the difference between right and wrong.

"I still don't know about that. It's a lil' suspect. You tryna get me killed."

"Fine, we'll just let Rico know you're a snitch, and the only reason you're out is because you agreed to help us bring him down. Let's see how long you live then."

Devon thought about hauling off and cracking the man over his head with his piece. He studied him for a quick moment. *Same height, same weight*, he thought. *The only thing that sets us a part is age and his badge. Hell, I ain't never killed a cop before, but I guess it'll feel the same as the others.*

Don wrote his cell number down on a torn piece of paper. "This is the number to call me on," he said to Devon. "Call me before you make any other cash transfers with Rico." He lowered his eyes. "Know we're watching you closely."

Just as Don finished his sentence, a blue and white NYPD tow truck pulled up abruptly and slammed the ignition into reverse. Without delay, the driver backed up, parking directly in front of Devon's Mustang. When Devon saw Don nod at the driver, he went ballistic.

"Hell, nah!" he shouted in rage.

"Hell, yeah," Don responded calmly. "This car is interfering with your job. Be a street worker, it makes better pictures." He laughed. "Besides, you gotta stay in town. No more Mass.!"

Devon nodded and walked off with Don, the tow truck, and his only transportation behind him. With his hands huddled deep inside his pockets, he resembled the loser of a battle being sent away. Devon, allowing himself to be punked, was either a sign of maturity or stupidity. He stopped momentarily, contemplating something drastic. He looked several yards behind him to see the tow truck lifting his car in the air. He shook his head and took two steps back. He took his hands from his pockets and grabbed hold of the handset of the payphone he stood in front of.

He dialed Carlie's cell number. No answer. Then he dialed the investigator's number. Instead of blasting off, he listened intently as Carlie's story unfolded. By the time Devon finished hearing about the police being at Carlie's house after she shot a woman, and that Kirk was somehow involved, he dropped the phone and sprinted down the street.

As Devon searched for a ride to the train station, he thought about what he'd been told in jail about Kirk trying to set Carlie up to get her money. Every cab that whipped by was occupied. He panicked, feeling like he needed to get to Carlie. She needed him.

Looking around like a man in search of a lost child, Devon spotted his potential ride. One block to his left, on a secluded street, loads of furniture covered the sidewalk. As the new homeowners struggled to carry a sofa up the twelve flights of stairs, Devon watched closely. The driver's seat to the U-Haul sat unoccupied. For minutes, he waited to see if anyone was on their way back out. Boldly, he broke out in a fast strut, headed to the truck. He wasn't sure if it was a good idea, but was ready for whatever happened.

Jumping in the truck, he looked up the flight of stairs to see if someone was looking. The door shut, the engine ignited, and the stolen U-Haul darted down the street, mixing into the middle of traffic. Devon headed toward the highway, with his foot smashing the pedal as far as it would go. Headed to Massachusetts, he hoped the police wouldn't stop him. Going back to jail wasn't an option, nor was keeping him away from Carlie.

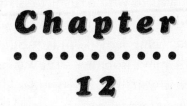

Chapter
12

On the way from the precinct, Carlie beamed inside at the way she handled Detective Travis Peters. She had been thrown questions out of the blue that shouldn't have been asked. Her skill as a lawyer definitely came in handy, as she flung questions back at the detective. The moment Carlie asked, shouldn't she have a lawyer present, the interrogation was over.

With her arms folded across her chest, she walked out the precinct with a little less confidence than normal. Simply put, it would take only one person to suspect that she shot China purposefully, and that would send her to prison for years. Not to mention if China died, the gas chamber.

Luckily, Detective Peters reported that China had lived, and was in the hospital in a deep coma. She had a thirty percent chance of making it. Being shot in the head meant two things. There was the possibility of her having severe brain damage, or one day waking up and telling exactly what happened inside of Carlie's house.

For Carlie, China waking up would be a catastrophe. She and Kirk were undercover suspects for now. And it didn't make matters any better that she was being watched from the window as she walked with a suspicious stride, looking back over her shoulder. With her baseball cap pulled low and her designer sweats, being ladylike was the furthest thing from her mind. For some reason, her strut was harder than before.

Without even watching, she paraded dead in the middle of the street like a mental patient, ignoring the horns honking her way. The plan was for her to wait for Kirk in the Starbucks across the street while he gave his statement. But patience had skipped town as jitters sparked through her body, thinking about the look on Kirk's face before she left. His attitude had changed overnight. Instead of catering to her every whim, he acted more in control and gave Carlie unrealistic instructions.

On one hand, she appreciated how he'd taken control of the situation, and coached her on what not to say during the questioning. But another part of her despised how he wouldn't allow any moves over the next few days without him. He insisted they needed to stick together until the police ruled them completely out as suspects.

Under normal circumstances, Carlie would've laughed at such a crazy request and told Kirk to go to hell. But strangely, she went along with everything he said. She couldn't believe he had even convinced her not to call her father.

While Carlie waited at a small table near the back of the coffee shop, visions of China's face flashed through her mind. Her frightening face and bright red lipstick, gave her goose bumps. Carlie wondered how she'd gotten into this situation. Obviously, Kirk was lying about some things. *What woman would come to another woman's house wearing a raincoat with nothing underneath? Maybe he was leading her on?*

Carlie flinched when the heavy hand gripped her shoulder. "You alright?"

"Yeah. I guess." Carlie hunched her shoulders. The anticipation was getting the best of her. "Well…"

"Well, I guess they asked me some of the same stuff they asked you," Kirk responded, without concern. He sat a tall cup of White Chocolate Mocha in front of Carlie.

"Like what?" she asked, with frustration in her eyes. Her hands clutched the drink. "Thanks." She sipped the drink like an alcoholic craving her favorite drink.

"They wanted to know if I really thought China was trying to rob you. I said yes." Kirk looked from side-to-side, like he had a secret to tell. "Then they asked why didn't she have a gun."

Carlie's eyes enlarged. "Damn, you're right. I never thought about it like that. Why was she there, Kirk?" Her tone changed.

"Why the hell you asking me?"

"You should know." Carlie folded her arms and twisted her lips. "Is there anything you want to tell me? That is, before the police dig deeper."

"Tell you what? You know I messed with China in the past."

"Oh, so now you wanna finally tell the truth? That's obvious, Kirk!" Carlie hit the table. "What other reason would she have to access my personal information, playing games with my phones, showing up at the airport, and the list goes on!" Carlie glanced to the left at a nosy woman staring them head on. "She didn't have a gun, Kirk! But she was naked!

Was she was there for you, or maybe down for a threesome?"

Kirk looked puzzled as he watched Carlie gulp the hot drink. "In case you didn't know, I'm stressed out too. I could be in just as much trouble as you."

"I'm not in trouble," she shot back. Just as Kirk gave her a funny look, she continued. "I have no idea what that look is all about, but I do know this."

"And what's that, Carlie?"

"She was your girlfriend. And she had a key to my house! How'd she get it? Hmm…I wonder, damn it!" Carlie surprised Kirk when she snapped her neck like a ghetto girl. That was so out of character for her. "The police said you were havin' some serious problems, and that she had called the police on you a few times before. They even said you two argued the night before she came to my house." Carlie gave Kirk the strangest look.

"What?" he asked, throwing up his hands. "That never happened. Who told you that?"

"Whatever." She threw her hands high in the air. "You just can't be trusted. You said you hadn't seen her since we came back from Jamaica."

"I didn't." Kirk lied with a straight face. He tried to pretend like he wasn't bothered by the information the police had given Carlie.

He wondered what kind of games they were playing. It was obvious they were playing them against each other. Kirk had heard about the police playing one suspect against another, but for now, it wasn't his major concern. He mustered up a smile, as he whipped out his stack of papers.

"What's all of this?" Carlie's hands opened wide.

"It's my life. Our life."

Carlie looked both puzzled and frustrated, as she recognized the name on the paperwork. She fumbled the legal size pages between her fingers. "Why are we talking about a car lot at a time like this?"

"I wasn't born with a silver spoon in my mouth," he said. "I've gotta make ends meet. You said you would sign. Now sign!" he yelled, handing Carlie the ballpoint pen.

Carlie took a deep breath before giving Kirk the bad news. "I can't."

"What the fuck?"

"It's my credit. You might fuck this deal up and leave me hanging."

"If I fuck up, the dealership becomes yours!"

"That's just it, Kirk. I don't want a car business. I already have a business. You should keep trying until you can get the loan on your own," she said with pity.

"China was going to help me," he shot back. Carlie's eyes widened. She had no idea where Kirk was going with this. "I hurt her heart when I dumped her for you, then I took her soul when I watched you shoot her. If she wasn't in the hospital about to die, I wouldn't have these problems!" Kirk stood up.

"You don't have any real problems. Now sit down." Kirk was certainly becoming a problem. Carlie had to think fast. She wasn't going to be blackmailed into signing for the loan.

"Yeah, I do have problems. The police think you shot China on purpose. And since I'm your man, I'm caught up in the middle." Kirk wrapped Carlie's hand around the pen and breathed closely into her face. "Sign," he spat.

Carlie's mind raced and her heart rate tripled. *What do I do?* she thought. *I didn't shoot China deliberately. I'm innocent.*

After all, she came into my home. What has Kirk been telling the police behind closed doors? I'm innocent.

"Sign, Carlie," he said with force.

Carlie fidgeted in her seat. $200,000, the loan amount, stared her in the face. She truly didn't want her name tied to any of Kirk's business deals. Whether it flourished or failed, she'd probably never see any of the money. Kirk was bad with finances, and it was obvious their relationship would soon be over. For now it was about who could be the most clever. Carlie leaned back, holding her chest, like she was having an anxiety attack.

"I can't," she said.

"Yes, you can!"

"No, what I mean is, I will. I just need some help. I'm having bad chest pains, and I might need to go to the hospital." Carlie lifted the pen slowly and held it in Kirk's direction.

He understood what she was asking for and placed his hand over hers. Within seconds, he assisted her with her stroke. Her name was quickly written sloppily across the signature line, but nonetheless, was there.

"All done," she said. "And don't forget my name goes on the lease for the lot?"

He stood, signaling that the meeting was over. "Partners," Kirk snickered, shaking Carlie's hand.

"Sure. I've gotta run to the office once I get myself together. You go ahead, I'll be okay."

Kirk checked his watch. "I'll meet you at your house by nine. If you start to feel worse, call me. You might need to see a doctor. You shouldn't be alone right now."

Carlie gave him a half smile. "Yeah, I guess I'll see you at nine," she said, as if it was killing her to agree. She paused for a moment, frozen in deep thought. "Thanks for everything," she smirked, before Kirk walked out.

* * *

As soon as Carlie opened the door to her office, the shouting began. "Just tell me what the hell is wrong with you? You can't be that stupid?"

Carlie took a deep breath, trying to figure out what to say first. Being screamed at like an elementary student was rare. "I…"

"I nothing. I shouldn't have to hear from the Chief of Police that I need to talk to my daughter. It's bad enough that he's on us for defending the guy who shot and killed his niece, but now you've shot a woman inside your home. Why in the hell didn't you call me?" Ricky stood firmly, with his hands deep in his pockets.

Carlie broke down. She had been through enough drama over the last month to last a lifetime. If she had called Ricky after the shooting, she wouldn't be in jeopardy of going to jail. His disapproving expression made her stutter as she spoke.

"I…d…d…d…don't…know…why I didn't call." Her palms pressed firmly against her flushed cheeks, while she paced the floor in a panic.

"I don't know why you do the crazy stuff you do. You just can't get it right. The Dupree case is our top priority. First, you're running out of town behind Kirk, and now you've shot a woman. She might die!"

"I was being robbed! Be thankful that I had a gun!"

"Umh," he retorted sarcastically. "It was registered, right?"

"Of course. Do you think I'm crazy?"

"Don't ask me that right now." Ricky shook his head. "If Kirk had been there, maybe this wouldn't have happened."

"He was there."

"Then why in the hell didn't he do something?" he questioned.

"By the time he got downstairs, I had already shot the lady."

"At least he can verify what happened."

Tears poured from her eyes like running water from a faucet. Carlie wanted to come clean, but couldn't. She didn't want to let her father down once again. She didn't think he could handle two failed relationships, even though this was all Kirk's fault. She wiped the dripping tears from her face.

Ricky thought about what he was putting his daughter through. She had possibly taken a life and was obviously traumatized. He remembered the awkward feeling of shooting someone for the first time, even though his was planned. He grabbed Carlie and pulled her close. Her upper body lay across his shoulders, as he patted her back like an obedient child.

"Carlie, forgive me. I'm just upset that all of this is happening. You know this isn't supposed to happen to people like us."

She sniffled. "I guess I now know how my client feels."

"Not yet. And unless you plan on being convicted, you won't."

She laughed hesitantly.

"Now, get yourself together and let's talk about the case.

We've got a meeting with the prosecutor and the judge in the morning. And the way I see it, there are two ways to get our man out of hot water."

Carlie didn't look shocked that Ricky was taking over. His stance reeked authority as he pulled out two big trays of paperwork and motioned for her to join him at the large round table.

"Jewell, come in here," he yelled like a father and not a seasoned lawyer.

The moment Jewell entered, both she and Carlie looked like new students on their first day of school. Ricky threw different folders toward them with all kinds of crazy instructions attached. "Now, it seems very strange to me that there were over twenty reports of domestic violence filed with the police over the last three years," he stated with a twisted look.

"That's not strange," Carlie said.

"Oh, yes it is. In most of these reports, Marcus was the one who called the police." Look at this one," Ricky said, showing Carlie a copy of one of the police reports. "Why would he beat her, then call the police?"

The thought of Marcus physically abusing his girlfriend made Carlie flinch. She believed that he didn't kill the woman, but couldn't understand why he didn't come clean about the previous beatings. Knowing that he was an abuser, all of a sudden made her feel differently about him. Yes, she was still his lead lawyer, and wanted to get him acquitted, but hoped that her personal feelings wouldn't interfere with how she tried the case. "Dad, look at this," she pointed to another document. "Saundra Kelly's father was a witness to the fight Marcus and Saundra had on 08-23-05. Jewell, send one of our investigators over to interview him," she ended.

"Sure thing," Jewell replied.

Ricky grinned. His baby girl was starting to come to her senses. He knew she had it in her, she just needed to get back on track. "Oh, you're not going to believe this piece of information," Ricky said like he was on to something.

By the time he shared the strange news with Carlie, they both felt like the case was taking a turn for the best. The next four hours were spent digging for missing information that needed to be uncovered. Marcus was obviously holding back on some very important information and Carlie was about to get to the bottom of it.

Chapter
• • • • • • • • • •
13

Carlie stepped out the doors of her office building short-ly after 9 p.m. After a grueling day of meetings with Ricky, she couldn't wait to get home. Stretching her shoulders, she looked to her left, then her right, in search of Kirk. Luckily, most businesses were closed after dark, which drove the majority of people away from the down town area shortly after work. Carlie hated the hustle and bustle during the day hours, and loved the moment of peace and crisp night air.

Just as Kirk had promised, he waited patiently across the street on the hood of his car. He knew when Carlie worked after dark, she needed to be picked up. The area was dimly lit, and pretty much abandoned at night. Carlie gave a life-less wave as she walked sluggishly in his direction, sizing him up. She'd thought about him often over the course of the day, and wished that he'd just go away for a few weeks. Now that Ricky was in town, everything was under control. No more questions from the police about China, and no more obsta-cles with the Dupree case.

Carlie froze as she was two steps away from Kirk. Her heart nearly burst through her chest. She watched her so-called boyfriend jump from the hood, and lean comfortably against the car. Her shortness of breath caught his attention. Kirk looked at her strangely, wondering why she was behaving like she'd seen a ghost. The shock of seeing Devon come up behind him, made her body react like an asthma patient. From that moment on, she could only point. But the warning was no good.

Devon's surprise visit caused the hairs on Kirk's chest to stand up straight. Devon snatched his gun from his waist with one hand, and plugged the stainless steel 9mm into Kirk's side. In the same breath, with the other hand, he grabbed Kirk's neck and applied unbearable pressure.

"Did you think I'd really let a punk mufucka like you slide?" Devon's intent was clear. Dressed for the occasion in an all black hoodie, his doo-rag and black Timberlands, he was thugged-out.

Kirk leaned back stiffly, catching a glance of Devon's expression. For the first time in years, he was face-to-face with his old road-dog. His body tilted even more, catering to Devon's pull.

"Hey, man. You don't wanna do this." Kirk spoke calmly, trying not to trigger any extra emotions.

"No, I do wanna do this, playa." Devon's rough demeanor was natural, but his time in prison had added extra fire.

Finally collecting herself, Carlie screamed, "No…please…Devon. No!"

Jealousy oozed through his pores. "You still checkin' for this nigga?" Devon questioned. He removed the gun from

Kirk's side and pressed it firmly to his temple, while looking at Carlie for an answer. "Huh?" he asked again.

"Oh, God! No!" Carlie bent over and clutched her stomach. She prayed someone would come by at that moment. But it was as if the whole street was deserted.

"Step back," Devon ordered, as Carlie stepped an inch closer.

She trembled with fear, but knew something had to be done. She could tell by his grimace that she was about to be a witness to a murder. She couldn't afford to have her name mixed up with another shooting. In the old days, she'd seen Devon rough people up thousands of times, but had never been a witness to his killings.

Carlie spoke slowly and seemed to be a bit out of it. "C'mon, Devon. Put the gun down!"

Just then, a pair of headlights came their way. Carlie lit up inside. She didn't want Devon to be locked up, but at least stopped. As she prepared to jump in front of the moving car to wave the driver down, her eyes widened. The dread-lock brotha behind the wheel bobbed his head to the loud reggae music, as a cloud of smoke was seen through the window. He zipped by like lightening, without even noticing them on the side of the street. Carlie stood distraught and shook her head.

"Okay, Devon. That's enough. Let him go!"

He laughed like a wild maniac. "I don't think so." Spit went from the tip of his tongue to the side of Kirk's cheek.

Carlie expected to see Kirk in a panic by now. Between the uninvited spit, and the sound of Devon cocking his gun back, the average person would've fainted. Instead, Kirk continued to wear his poker-face, as sweat poured from his forehead. She looked at them both intently. Seeing the only two men she'd ever had a serious relationship with, in a life or death setting, was difficult. One could be physically abusive, yet protective. While the other was a womanizer, a liar, and mentally abusive at times. *Carlie wanted neither of them to die.*

Kirk decided against any more words or reasoning. He wasn't ready to meet his maker. He made eye contact and looked deep into Devon's eyes, trying to figure out if his boy would really take him out. They'd been through a lot in their younger days, and watched each other's back many times before. Kirk reminisced about the time Devon shot up an entire block, helping him out of a bad situation. He had visited a female friend, and thirty minutes into the visit, her angry boyfriend showed up waving a gun. The deranged man was just about to handle Kirk when Devon showed up and saved the day.

Kirk also thought about the times when he had to save Devon's ass. On many occasions, Devon would drink himself into a drunken state, only to catch stares from street thugs who wanted to see him dead. Devon's drug business thrived in the late nineties, and everyone wanted a piece of it. Kirk would guard him like a junkyard dog, making sure he was safe. Although he hated actually putting people to sleep, he had performed his share of pistol whippings on Devon's behalf. Visions of the two of them laughing flashed through Kirk's mind.

He even thought about the nights when he and Devon would sleep in the car all night outside of Carlie's house, making sure no one went in or out. Even though he hated spying on her, he knew Devon depended on him. Kirk wanted to speak up about what he was thinking, but decided to keep quiet. After all, he destroyed the loyalty between them when he slept with Carlie.

Several minutes had gone by before Carlie thought about dialing 911 on her phone. It was her last resort.

Just as she reached for the phone, she heard Devon ask, "You tryna set Carlie up?"

Kirk didn't respond. He was puzzled.

Devon nudged him. "You heard me. I know what you told the police. I got peeps everywhere."

Carlie looked to Kirk for answers. "What's he talking about Kirk?" She backed away like someone was planning on attacking her. Her head moved back and forth at a fast pace.

"I know some folks in the department. They say your man here," he pointed to Kirk, "told 5.0 you shot his girl on purpose." Devon didn't want to tell Carlie that the investigator he hired from New York was feeding him information, and that the price was rising more and more.

Kirk felt hollow inside. He wasn't sure how much Devon knew, and he damn sure couldn't figure out how he got his information. "Devon, you got it confused," he said, in a guilty tone. He swallowed hard.

"Yeah, just like I had it all confused when you left town with my loot. Just like I had it confused when you tried your best to help the prosecutors get me a nice long, fuckin' sentence!" Devon pressed Kirk's head firmly up against the window. "And what about when you fucked my woman? Did I get that wrong too? Huh?"

"Nah, man. It ain't like that."

"Give me one good reason why I shouldn't blast you?" Devon roared. His voice grew angrier by the minute.

Kirk tried not to show any emotion. "Don't do this,

Devon."

"You realize what you did, playa."

"Man, I got the money I owe you!" Kirk's voice grew frantic. He knew Devon well enough to know he was about to pull the trigger.

"It's not just about the money! Besides, you ain't got it, broke-ass, nigga!" Devon kicked at his feet.

"I just ran into some money. You gotta believe me," Kirk begged.

"Let's talk about how you been tellin' niggas how you got a girl that you gon' take to the cleaners." Devon glanced over at Carlie's sunken in face. "People talk. I knew when I was locked up what you was doin'."

"Look, let me start by paying you back."

Carlie had heard enough about how Kirk betrayed her and his plea to make things right with Devon. *He probably wants to pay with the money I just signed for*, she thought. Without fear of the gun, she walked right up to Devon and placed her hand near Kirk's temple.

"He's not worth it," Carlie said, with a clear mind.

Devon looked at her strangely. His eyes asked the question, me or him?

"Let him go before I'm wanted as a suspect in his murder. There's no telling what he's said to the cops." Carlie led the way, signaling Devon to follow. "Let's go before you get locked up again," she said, in a controlling manner.

Devon's first reaction was to finish Kirk off anyway. He owed him big time, but Carlie's freedom was on the line. He loved her deeply and couldn't cope with seeing anything else happen to her. If he took Kirk out at that moment, she'd definitely become a primary suspect.

"You just got blessed with a gift," Devon said, releasing Kirk. He backed away slowly, with his gun still pointed. "You do her any harm at all, then just count yourself dead."

Kirk didn't make any moves, and not a word left from his lips. He watched Carlie turn the corner, walking slightly ahead of Devon. As soon as Devon turned the corner, Kirk took out his phone and dialed as quickly as he could.

* * *

Fifteen minutes later, Carlie and Devon were in a cab on their way to Carlie's house. After several minutes of debate, she finally agreed to let Devon see her home safely. He filled her in on the details, and convinced her that Kirk was devious and that she wasn't completely safe at the moment.

It shocked Carlie to hear Devon say, "Maybe you should call your father." Devon had expressed his hate for Ricky a hundred times over in the past. But if it meant Carlie being taken care of, he was willing to put their differences aside.

Deciding whether to trust Devon or Kirk was a hard choice, but at the moment, Kirk couldn't be trusted. All of the pieces were beginning to fit. Kirk didn't want to be a suspect in China's case at all. He knew Carlie shot China on purpose with her second shot and he would tell the police if he had to.

"Devon, what made you come here?" she asked.

"You."

"No seriously." She tried to hold it back, but her faint blush peeked through. "This is too much drama for you to be around. If you get caught up in any of this, you're goin' back to jail. I can handle myself."

"I found out you got yourself in a lil' trouble."

"How'd you know?" she asked with concern.

"I got eyes and ears everywhere. Just look at me." He pointed to his grimy clothes. "I had this on for two days, lookin' out for you. Making sure nothin' happened to you."

An eerie feeling crept through Carlie's body. His statement reminded her of the old days. "My dad is in town, he's watching out for me."

"I know, but I wanna be the one who looks out for you. I wanna be the one you call when you're in trouble," he whispered, as his arm slid behind her back. His warm breath brushed her earlobe and sent sparks through her body.

"Devon, don't start," she demanded. Her hand smacked at his arm like a fly swatter.

"Just give us a chance."

"There is no *us*."

"Look me in my face and tell me you don't love me." Devon gave the cab driver a deadly look, after realizing he was deep into their conversation.

Carlie turned to avoid Devon's gaze. She looked out the window, hoping the cabby would step on it. *Ten more minutes*, she thought. It was already planted in her head that when the cab pulled up, she was hopping out, not even giving Devon a chance to walk her to the door. She still had the hots for him, and didn't want to chance him coming inside. The only thing she needed at the moment was a 1000-milligram of Tylenol.

"I'm waitin'," Devon said, in a clear-cut tone.

"I love you," she finally said. "Okay, I said it. I'm just not in love with you. I hate what you stand for when it comes to relationships."

"What do you mean?"

"You want to control your women. Or have you forgotten? You know, beat me when I'm not following your lead. Put me in choke holds!" Frustrated, Carlie held her hand above her forehead.

"Carlie, c'mon. I've matured. I'm done with all of that."

"Yeah, me too," she smirked. "Devon, I'm content."

Carlie's definite tone shot through him like a knife. He expected her to feel the same way about him as he did about her. He decided to try one last move as they approached Carlie's block. He knew she could never deny his kisses. They'd locked lips many times in the past to reconcile their relationship. *Carlie couldn't deny his tongue action*, he thought.

Just as he leaned in for the kill, Devon spotted an undercover police car. He knew makes and models like the back of his hand. One officer sat in the car located three doors from Carlie's house. Devon signaled for Carlie to look when he saw the detective walking toward her front door. Her mouth hung low when she spotted Devon's concern. She could recognize Detective Peter's afro anywhere.

Noticing her frightened stare, Devon grabbed Carlie and hugged her with a weird tightness. He instantly tapped the driver on the shoulder. "Keep it movin'," he gestured.

"I thought this was the street?"

"Nah. She's goin' with me." When Devon felt a tear on his chest, he tightened his grip. His woman needed him.

"So, where to?" the cabby asked.

Devon looked down at Carlie, who had her head buried in his chest. He stared at her for a moment, then at the driver. "The Downtown Hilton," he said.

Carlie never looked up until the cab stopped in front of the hotel. A gallon of tears had already fallen during the thirty-minute ride, and more was sure to come. Carlie's life was virtually falling apart right in front of her eyes. She grabbed her purse, wiped her eyes, and followed Devon into the hotel.

By the time she reached the counter, Devon was in control and doing all of the talking. She stood back biting her nails, like a young girl on vacation with her parents. In spite of all her problems, she smiled inside when Devon pulled out a wad of hundreds. For the first time in years, she was being spoiled again.

"One room or two," Devon asked, catching Carlie off guard.

"Uhh…"

"It's whatever you want, Carlie."

She shrugged her shoulders, as a funny feeling fizzed inside. "I guess it doesn't matter." Carlie thought about pulling Devon close right there in the lobby. A tall, handsome roughneck, protecting her through the night was just what the doctor ordered. She just didn't want to make it seem like she wanted him.

"One room," Devon said to the clerk. He looked back at Carlie and smiled that smile that had always driven her crazy.

Chapter
• • • • • • • • • •
14

Kirk watched a dark-skinned little guy with braids run from the front of the building toward the basketball courts. He squinted, checking to see if it was Snake. He could've sworn it was him, and that he had deliberately ignored the hand signal. Quickly he exited the car upset, and headed on a wild goose chase. His plan was to pick up the money Snake owed him from weeks ago, pay Rico when he arrived, and hit Snake with more product to sell. Money was getting tight.

Over the last few days, Kirk had spent hundreds of dollars staying at hotels and needed some money to hold him over. The loan Carlie signed for was scheduled to be finalized and deposited into Kirk's account in the next few days.

The money Snake was making him was peanuts compared to the money that would come in from the car sales. Two hundred thousand wasn't a lot of start up cash, but Kirk had already begun to spend the money before he got it. He'd placed an order for two luxury BMWs with low-miles, and three Mercedes Benzes, to be the first on his lot. Kirk had convinced the owner of the space to allow him to sign a new lease without Carlie's name on it. He grinned at his shrewd thought. *It would be his and his only.*

Trying to camouflage himself between a group of guys up to no good, Snake saw Kirk headed his way. He darted behind a huge blue dumpster, sure that Kirk hadn't seen him. Snake was shocked to even see Kirk. Devon had assured him that he would be handled. Unless he was a ghost, his new boss hadn't lived up to his part of the bargain.

With his body in a crouched position, he hid, giving Kirk enough time to leave the neighborhood. He wasn't afraid of Kirk, he just didn't want an unnecessary beef. He breathed heavily while Kirk kicked it with a few dudes nearby. They talked for a brief moment, shook hands, and departed ways like he was leaving. Just when Snake thought it was over, Kirk walked right up behind him.

Snake didn't appear fearful, just shocked. He knew Kirk wasn't the gangsta type, but would still expect his loot. When he realized he was caught, a fake smile spread across his face.

"You ain't see me looking for you?" Kirk asked, in a fiery tone.

"Nah, dog," Snake answered, which was a bold face lie. He stood to his feet and made a jittery motion with his hands.

It was obvious Kirk was being ducked. He had called Snake numerous times over the past few days, and didn't get any return calls. He figured he didn't have all of his money, but they had been doing business long enough to cut him some slack. The problem was that Kirk had to pay Rico something. He hadn't been around in a while and didn't want that beef at all. He'd promised to meet Rico shortly after 8 p.m., which meant he only had an hour to round up what Snake was missing.

"How much you got?" Kirk finally blurted out, with his hand extended.

Snake had a stupid look on his face, as he slid his hands between his braids. He hesitated like he didn't have the money. Then it hit him. He thought of the most reasonable explanation.

"Dog, the police raided us the other night."

"Oh yeah," Kirk responded. He could smell the weed on Snake's breath, and wondered if his high was keeping him from thinking clearly. "When was the raid?"

"The other night." His hand gestures went wild, his nervousness clear.

"They took it all?"

"I had a lil' bit in the crib, but some guys messed me up with some of that money too."

"Don't let me find out you bought a new grill for your mouth." Although Kirk meant it to be a joke, there was no laughter. He wanted his money. "So, when you plan on getting my paper right? I got people to answer to." Kirk's frustration was becoming clear, which was a first for Snake.

"I got you, dog. Don't worry." His hands opened and closed even more.

"I know you got something. Gimme what you can for now. A brotha is hurting."

Snake's face turned red as a beet. He couldn't believe Kirk asked him for any of the money. Every since Devon told him he wouldn't have to pay Kirk, he'd been splurging nightly at the clubs, buying bottles of champagne and pimping the ladies. He thought about the small knot of money in his pants pocket and hoped that Kirk didn't notice the bulge. He mentally counted the twenties and hundreds in his pocket, trying to decide if he should give him a few dollars, or chill until he was erased from the picture. For Snake the word *loyalty* didn't exist. He was only partial to *green. It's a dirty game,* he thought.

He also had visions of the thick honey he promised to wine and dine later that night, and decided against giving up any money, not one dollar. Females were his weakness, and everyone knew it.

"Look, dog, I'm messed up right now. Give me a day or so, I'll call you."

"Sure you will."

"What's that supposed to mean?"

Snake was skinny as a rail. If he wanted to, Kirk could break him in half like a toothpick. Instead he nodded. "I know you'll call. I don't got you as being a cruddy dude. I'll be waiting."

Under normal circumstances, Kirk would've been pissed that his money was being fucked over. He calmed down, confident that he'd be paid by Snake soon. He'd been working with him for over two years without having any problems, so he figured there wasn't a need to overreact. For now, he needed to decide what he was going to tell Rico. The meeting was set, and the money wasn't right.

"I'll get at you," Kirk ended, extending his fist out for a pound. "You put me in a bind, but I'll be alright," he said, throwing a guilt trip on Snake. His mind raced, thinking of anyone he could round up a few thousand from in a hurry. He came up with zero. Kirk had to laugh at how things were going down. Nothing was working for him. Devon was out to get him, his relationship with Carlie was pretty much over, some of his deals with his car lot had gone wrong, and now Snake was holding back on his loot.

Snake felt a tiny smidgen of guilt for dogging Kirk out like that. He stood with his arms folded as he watched him walk away. *Damn, I'm cool with Kirk in all, but I'm cooler with Benjamin and Andrew.* He smiled, thinking about the dollars in his pocket, trying to remember the Presidents on each.

"Damn, I should've stayed my black ass in school," he joked.

* * *

From the moment Kirk left Snake, until the time he saw Rico step from his SUV, the camera continued to snap pictures. The undercover cameraman moved steadily back and forth, securing perfect shots without being seen.

Rico strutted up to Kirk with his four hundred dollar shades on, like he owned a fortune 500 company. Behind him, his three burly protectors stood close enough to make a move if anything happened to him.

No sooner than the two men greeted each other with a stiff, quick brotherly hug and handshake, Kirk started with his plea.

"Man, I ain't even gonna pretend. Some of my paper got fucked up. I don't got your money."

Rico's pleasant attitude disappeared from his face. Kirk was already considered the weakest link. Out of all of the people who he sold to, Kirk was the slowest, and now he didn't have the little bit of money he owed. Rico held his arms open wide.

"What you want me to do? I gotta eat just like you."

"I know. I'm gonna pay you, I just need a few days."

"Is a few days really gonna do you some good? I don't have time for games or lies," he said, in a matter-of-fact tone.

"That's all I need." Kirk motioned like he really meant it. "Snake and a few other cats got some paper for me."

Rico frowned. He knew Snake had paid Devon over six thousand within the last week, and had been selling like crazy for him since Devon offered him extra money on every package. Since Snake was keeping more money for himself, he had tripled the amount of his normal sales. Now that Snake was working with Devon, there was no chance of Kirk getting paid, and Rico knew it.

"Look, don't confuse my money with who owes you. I need mine regardless."

Kirk started having crazy thoughts. He thought about Snake wilding out, spending up his money, and Rico wanting blood. "You think you could front me a quarter or two?"

Rico played Kirk's words over again in his head. He knew desperation was kicking in. He calculated what Kirk already owed him and what his balance would be on the new powder.

"Fine, I'll have my man right there meet you here with it in a 'bout ten minutes."

Kirk smiled inwardly as Rico walked away. "You a good dude, Rico!" he shouted.

"You too," he responded. "Don't let me down."

Inside, Rico grinned. Kirk wasn't rough at all, so if he didn't pay, he'd easily take his car to the chop shop and sell the parts for more money than he owed.

Chapter

· · · · · · · · · ·

15

When Ricky's answering service picked up, Carlie's heart thumped. How could she tell her father where she was or, for that matter, who she was with? The progress made on the case the day before had made Ricky extremely happy, and now, here she was about to ruin it all.

She'd finally gotten enough nerve to tell him she was taking a break from the case and work altogether, but the sound of his voice recording, made her lose what confidence she'd gained. She knew he would hit the roof, but what could she do? Mentally, her mind wasn't prepared to take on any work.

In light of her problems, her face still managed to glow with a smile that hadn't been seen in years. While she lay cuddled in bed naked, beneath the thick white sheets, she giggled at the thought of being pampered. She looked around at the clothes scattered about the floor, and wondered if the linen draped food cart was her reward.

Devon was obviously nowhere in sight, but the tray filled with melons, bananas and strawberries, caught her attention.

She leaned over from the bed, just enough to pull off the silver top covering the plate. In an instant, the smell of the pecan waffles and smoked bacon hit her in the face. Carlie noticed the delivered breakfast was set for one, and a note lay next to the pitcher of juice. At that moment, she wondered what actually happened last night?

She grabbed the note in anticipation, and grinned widely like a schoolgirl. She shook her head at the nice gesture of Devon's breakfast in bed, and grabbed the note that insinuated there was more to come. She smiled showing every dimple on her face, and every tooth in her mouth as she read:

Hey sexy,

You know I hated leavin' your fine ass. It took everything in me not to climb on top of you this morning and show you what we been missing. You let me know if anybody fucks with you while I'm gone; I mean anybody- the bell-cap, the room service guy, or even the damn maid. Make sure you eat. You gotta start taking care of yourself. Better yet, leave all of that to me. Be a good girl and eat all of your food (smile). But make sure you eat the fruit I ordered for you. They say certain fruits bring out the freak in you. See you when I get back.

Carlie sat amazed at how manipulative Devon could be. He had always been confident that he knew how to please her and any other woman. He knew exactly what to do to string his women along, and Carlie was now caught in his trap once again.

She looked around, feeling a sense of peace. Although she cried half the night, and only had the clothes that were spread across the floor, and the shoes under the bed; the high ceilings and top-notch suite at the Hilton was treating her good. While not as spacious as her house, the suite had enough amenities to keep her from wanting to go home. Soon she had dozed back off to sleep.

* * *

Three hours later, with arms folded, Carlie had developed an attitude by the time Devon walked through the door. He joked, "Honey, I'm home."

Carlie was quiet. She yawned and checked the clock. She wore an embarrassed look, like a hooker left to be alone after a rough night. With a long pause and the covers pulled above her nose, she finally spoke. "Where you been?"

Devon loved the comment. "Worried, huh?"

"Not really. It's just that you got me locked up in this hotel, waiting for you. Your note said you'd be right back."

"You could've left. It's a free world," he said, obviously feeling himself. Devon smiled, leaning into her face.

He sat on the side of the bed, making his move. His warm lips landed on hers and rested like they were waiting for some action. Devon wanted Carlie to make the first move.

"I didn't have any clothes," she mumbled, while his lips continued to smother hers.

His close presence made her feel giddy inside. Besides, it

was apparent that he had come across some new clothes. Devon looked good in his brown expensive-looking attire, which Carlie would've handpicked herself, and a sexy leather suede jacket to match. The smell of his cologne had her magnetized, like a bee chasing honey.

"I told you I'd look out for you." Without moving his body, his right arm reached to the floor and pulled out of nowhere two large bags filled with clothes.

"But I didn't need all of this," Carlie jumped, freeing herself from his grip. "How come you got so many outfits? You act like I'm never going home."

Devon paused like he wanted to say something else, but instead, he said, "I just thought it would be a nice surprise. And it worked." He nodded. "I haven't seen a smile on your face since we've been together."

"What do you mean together?" she questioned. Carlie knew Devon was controlling, and she didn't want to be labeled as *his woman* again, just yet.

"You know what I mean. Since I got out the joint."

Carlie rummaged through the bags like a teenager during back to school shopping. Her eyes feasted on jeans filled with rhinestones and fancy embroidery, along with the latest hard to get shirts. She flung the items from the bags one by one, catching a glimpse of Devon's enjoyment. Within moments, the bed was covered with fancy new underwear and the best bras money could buy, everything she needed. Just when she thought Devon had outdone himself, another huge box appeared.

"Boots for me," she said, looking at the picture on the side of the box.

"Did you think I forgot your fetish for shoes? We'll get

more later."

Speechless, she shook her head. Being showered with multiple gifts reminded her of the old days, the days when Devon would show up with Rolex watches, designer handbags, and hard to come by shoes. Although Carlie was now making her own money, there was something special about Devon's money. It spent better.

She remembered the time when he bought her a brand spanking new Benz. Not the kind her girlfriends would get as gifts and call it new, even though it would have 30,000 miles plus on it. It was the kind that made you feel like a queen sliding down in the seat. Devon was known to be a big spender and he spent his money the right way.

Carlie was ready to dash into his arms and rip his pants off. *This is how a girl should be treated*, she thought. He had his misfortunes and faults in life, but seemed to be the only man who'd ever truly satisfied her. She wished they could erase all the negatives from the past, so she could call Ricky to ask for his blessings. Her father wanted the best for her, but he would never accept Devon as a son-in-law.

"Hey, sit back a moment," Devon ordered. He removed the shirt from Carlie's hand that she'd already declared as her favorite.

Carlie could tell that what he had to say was well thought out. His demeanor had changed from easy going to serious.

"What is it?" she asked with concern.

"I wanna come clean." He paused for a moment and lowered his head. "I know in the past I watched you a lil' too closely, and didn't give you space. Believe me when I say I'm a changed man." He grabbed her hand, squeezing each finger.

Oh, shit! she thought, *not a proposal.*

"I had you followed," he blurted out.

"What the fuck?" Carlie snatched her hand back and leaned against the headboard. "Just when I thought you changed!"

"I have. Believe me."

"Whatever, Devon."

"No, seriously. I had you followed to keep an eye on you. You lucky I did, 'cause the investigator I hired is in good with the detectives on your case."

Her eyebrows creased. "The Dupree case?" Even though she was pissed, Devon's information seemed important.

"No, the shootin'."

"Tell me," she said, sitting up.

"The detectives at your door last night were probably there to tell you the latest news."

"What? Tell me now!" She could tell from Devon's expression that it wasn't good at all.

"China woke up."

Carlie just knew she was having a massive heart attack. Her mouth opened wide and her eyes bulged. "What? When?"

"Last night. And not only that."

"Don't tell me!" She held her chest. This time it wasn't an act like she'd put on for Kirk.

"She's pregnant. The detective is willin' to bet its Kirk's."

Carlie's jaw hung low. "Pregnant?" she asked, just to be sure she wasn't hearing things.

"No doubt. You heard me."

"The baby didn't die? That's crazy."

"For now. So Kirk might be a daddy in a few months."

That lying motherfucker, she thought. *Was it more important to be afraid that China would try to accuse her of attempted murder? Or should her attention be targeted at getting back at Kirk?* She sat quietly, not wanting Devon to know her thoughts about Kirk being a big phony. She was more hurt that he was playing her, as opposed to the fact he was cheating. But for now she had to play it cool in front of Devon.

"Why would they want to tell me?" she finally asked. "That's Kirk's business." Her shoulders moved in a nonchalant motion.

"They were comin' to question you a lil' more. You and Kirk's stories don't match up. You know how cops roll. Sneaky." He bit at his lip. "I think you should stay away a lil' longer. You know, let the smoke clear." He leaned in closer, noticing that her eyes were watery. Her face was still covered with dried tears from the night before.

Devon didn't have a clue about the issue that made her cry the most, but the distressed look on her face showed that it was really affecting her. Inside, Carlie exploded thinking about China telling the police that she tried to kill her. She could picture her saying Kirk knew she was there, or that they set her up to be killed. The question — would the police buy it?

Carlie thought a little bit more, and realized that maybe China wasn't well enough to talk to the police yet. Maybe she would realize that she broke into her house, and could potentially be arrested for breaking and entering. Carlie was in such a vulnerable state. Thoughts bounced around in her head like a ping-pong ball.

She leaned forward on Devon's chest, while he squeezed her thighs for comfort. His eyes darted down to her exposed tits peeking out the covers. His first lick warned her about what was coming next. Convincing herself to say no, she sat stiffly.

Carlie shivered at the thought of feeling him again. She desperately needed a tune-up, hell an engine overhaul, something to take her mind away from it all. Her life was becoming more and more unpredictable, but her hunger for a good sex life was clear.

The night before, Devon struggled, almost giving himself blue balls holding Carlie through the night, while trying not to make the first move. It was pure torture. He wasn't about to let that happen again. Five years of back-up began to pump forcefully through his blood, and stabbed at his mind. While his hard-on stood out like a sore thumb, he was determined to show Carlie he was there for her and pretended sex wasn't important.

Half a second passed, and both Carlie and Devon were nearly exploding. Carlie couldn't pretend anymore. All in all, she loved him and always had. She finally released the covers with ease, giving Devon the go-ahead signal. She wanted to play hard to get, but the wetness from her panties ruled that out. The only thing to do now was make the best of it.

"You sure this is what you want?" he whispered.

Shyly, she nodded yes.

"Take my jacket off," he ordered.

That's new, she thought. He was always the more aggressive one. Carlie pushed the jacket back to his shoulders and Devon finished the rest.

"You want the rest of this to stay on?" he teased. His reverse psychology was working. He took his time undressing right before Carlie's eyes, while she mentally drooled inside.

Before she knew it Devon had stripped down, butt naked, exposing his chiseled body and firm chest. He seemed to tease her on purpose as he stood in front of her with his dick swinging. Devon stared at her with a lustful look, but made no moves.

Carlie's heart thumped while she waited for him to make his move. She threw the covers back even further, and posted her legs in a welcoming position. She felt like she'd missed out on so much pleasure over the last five years, and wanted him badly, but the wait was too long.

Out of character, Carlie quickly pulled her fitted tank above her head to show Devon she was ready. He moved in slowly, but dug the palm of his hand deep into her panties. Immediately, his touch drove her wild. Carlie twitched and became soaked instantly. Devon knew it and decided to make sure she'd want him forever. His warm body slid on top and covered Carlie completely. The skin to skin feeling felt so good. His warm body had obviously already turned her on, but when his lips sucked the juices from her mouth she went wild.

Damn, she thought. Crazy-n-Love. She shoved her tongue deep into his mouth and held Devon's lips captive while she went crazy. Aggressively, she licked his insides from his gums down to his throat. Her body moved like a horny dog in heat as she gripped the back of Devon's butt pulling him close.

Devon knew Carlie was ready for penetration, but wanted his first piece of ass since his release to be spectacular. He grabbed Carlie's tank and wrapped it around her eyes as a blindfold. The last thing she saw were his firm shoulders just as everything went dark. She didn't know what to expect next. Devon was about do something unforgettable. He started by using his left hand to massage Carlie's erect nipples. By the time his right hand worked her throbbing clit, it felt like twelve sensual hands were all over her body working many spots at the same time.

Devon lifted his body slightly and leaned off the bed just a bit. Carlie expected to hear the buzzing sound of a battery operated toy next. But, a cold sensation spread through her body. The feel of melted ice between Devon's lips licked her all over and sent her mind into erotic thoughts she'd never considered before. Just when she thought it was over, Devon has sculpted a piece of ice with his mouth and inserted it inside Carlie.

After minutes of pleasurable play-time with the ice, Devon yanked Carlie's body into the perfect position. The moment she felt his hardness, her legs spread as wide as they could. She got just what she wanted when he thrust himself into her wetness. Carlie screamed at the first plunge. *It had never felt so good.*

It didn't take long for her legs to be wrapped around the upper part of his back. Her hips rose and lowered right along with his as she grinded rhythmically with Devon. Within minutes, Carlie was in the zone. Her moans were heard from one end of the 7th floor to the other. For Devon, it was perfect, just as he'd planned. His cum was ready to escape , but he was holding on for dear life.

"Devon!" she called out.

"Ah..." he moaned. Ah... was all he could say.

Carlie called his name once more. But still no words that made sense were heard. At the same time, she gripped underneath the headboard, to keep her head from suffering a concussion. When Devon gripped her ankles, she let out a loud scream as he pumped with harder thrust. The more he pumped the better it felt. Carlie gripped the headboard even tighter, using every muscle in her fingers. Her orgasm was slipping through as she yelled, "Yes!!!!!! Devon !!!!!! Yes!!!!!!" Without holding anything back, she rocked the bed with all her might. Anything Devon wanted at that moment, he could get.

Devon lowered the upper part of his body and stuttered softly in her ear, "You...you...you... feel so... so... damn good!"

Carlie was amazed at the rough yet passionate sex they shared. She was ready to go on for hours making up for lost time. But Devon couldn't take any more. He grunted loudly and acted as if he was having a convulsion. He released five years of frustration as he held Carlie tight. Devon looked into her eyes realizing he'd started something that he definitely intended on finishing.

Before the end of the night, the two sat in bed talking as if they were together for the first time. Devon talked about private moments in jail, while Carlie professed apologies for dealing with Kirk. Everything went well until she mentioned that she'd just signed for a $200,000 loan for Kirk. Devon went ballistic, and the night ended with yet another price on Kirk's head.

Chapter
• • • • • • • • • •
16

Carlie's mouth went dry. She could barely swallow as she watched Devon act like a maniac. For starters, she wasn't sure how he had convinced her to leave town and go with him to New York. Her job, her life, everything she owned was back at home, including leaving Ricky in charge of the case. Yet, she stood and watched with her arms folded while Devon trashed Kirk's work in progress. A part of her liked his payback, and this was just the beginning.

Although his office was half complete, the boxes that once decorated the floor were now kicked about the room.

"That's enough, Devon!" she finally yelled. "Let's go."

The dealership hadn't officially opened yet, but Devon found a way inside. The secretary had only showed up for one day to set up the computer, and to start working on the filing system. Devon had cased the place earlier, and knew Kirk was expecting a big turn out for his grand opening.

Carlie stood back like a smart partner in crime, while Devon smashed his fist at the framed pictures of luxury cars.

Glass flew everywhere, causing her to flinch, but she was sure to touch nothing. She glanced toward the door once more, praying that he was ready to go. But no deal, he had so much more to do.

Devon fixed his eyes on a huge framed picture of Kirk standing in front of the car lot. He stared at the photo, wondering what Carlie had seen in him. What made her want to be with a stocky, curly-head dude without any guts? It was almost as if she settled for second best. Devon was the one with the balls. He was the one with street smarts, the one who could protect her. Kirk was a plain follower, trying to be a Devon.

At the sound of his twelve and a half shoe crushing the broken glass from the frame into tiny pieces, Carlie figured enough was enough. She watched Devon's veins throb through the side of his face, wondering why he was so angry. Yes, Kirk had done a lot, but Devon really wanted to do something bad.

"Yeah, just what I'm lookin' for," Devon said sweating.

"Well, get it and let's go," Carlie said, anxious to leave. She rubbed her shoulders, still looking around the small office.

Devon stared at the long black book and smiled. He took two steps in Carlie's direction, giving her a sense of relief, then stopped in his tracks. He slammed the book on the desk, opened to the first page, and grabbed a pen.

"What are you doing?" Carlie asked, standing directly behind him.

"I'm writin' us a check." He shot her a deranged look and winked.

"From Kirk's account?"

"It's your money!"

"Let me handle the loan situation the legal way. I'll get my money back, one way or another."

"Fuck legal!" Devon shouted at Carlie, like she was the enemy. "That ain't gon' do nothin' but get you bad credit. We gon' do it my way, you feel me?" His hand worked fast, while he glanced at Carlie to make sure she was falling in line. Before he knew it, the words twenty thousand were written across the check.

"Who's going to sign the check?" she asked softly. She was itching to just come out with a sarcastic comment like, *what stupid bank is going to cash that damn check?*

"We gon' make that mufucka sign it. In blood if we have to! You feel me?"

"What is twenty thousand going to do anyway?"

"It's a start. He probably ran through all the money by now. He's a nigga that you gotta slow walk. Bounce on him weekly. You feel me?"

Carlie shook her head in agreement. She didn't want to go along with it, but for now, whatever it took to get Devon to leave would be fine. There was no way she'd stand before Kirk and ask him to sign a stolen check.

For some reason, she felt like she'd found herself right back in the same situation from years ago, following behind a man who made crazy decisions. One thing was for sure, she wasn't cashing that check. She had plans of dealing with Kirk on her own.

The sound of distant sirens sent Devon into a craze, and made Carlie antsy.

"Fuck, fuck, fuck," he chanted.

He grabbed his frantic woman by the hand, as her eyes

widened, and headed toward the door. His thoughts bounced uncontrollably back and forth. The decisions were deep. He wanted badly to smash up a few cars on the way out, but did-n't want to chance being caught with Carlie around.

His walk gained an instant lean, like he was ready for a riot. Carlie followed quickly behind as Devon kicked open the back door. Once outside, he turned in search of the cops. The sounds were still heard, but not one person was in sight. Devon realized the police were never coming for them. He decided to double-back around to the front. Carlie pulled at him like a contestant in a tug-of-war game.

"No, let's go," Carlie said.

Devon couldn't resist. Pow. Pow Pow. Three shots rang out, flattening the tires of a shiny four-door Lexus.

* * *

As soon as Devon got the chance, he dropped Carlie off at the cleanest hotel he could find near Harlem. His next stop was to go see Don. He'd left numerous shrewd written threats at his efficiency, saying the sheets in his jail cell were ready. Devon wasn't about to be on the run, so it was time to pay the piper.

The set up was already arranged. Like clockwork, Devon met the team at an old abandoned building on 116th and Lennox Avenue, around the corner from Amy Ruth's Chicken and Waffles. He looked over his shoulder nervously as he entered the chained gate, realizing there weren't any familiar faces. He was skeptical, but no other options came to mind.

Looking ahead, the darkness nor the unknown undercover officers, really scared him. But the idea of what he was about to do sent a bad feeling to his gut. It was one thing to be a snitch on the stand or behind bars, but another to look somebody in the face, knowing you're taking them down.

"You all set, Devon," a short white officer asked, emerging from the huddle. "I'm Agent Chaney, but just plain old Chaney will do." He extended his hand.

You could tell he was about business. He maintained a straight, no-nonsense face and never paid attention to any of Devon's ignorant expressions. Chaney grabbed a roll of tape from the duffle bag and held it out in front of Devon.

"The best way not to get caught-up is to tape this little box under your scrotum."

"Scrotum?"

"Yep, your dick, pecker, or whatever you call that thing."

Devon looked at the officer like he was crazy. Before he could speak again, Chaney put him in his place. "I don't give a fuck if you wear it on your nipples. I'm not in jeopardy of going back to jail, you are! Now drop your pants and put the shit on before we have a faggot come strap it on for you."

Devon was outnumbered as the officers giggled from behind. He couldn't understand why so many men were looking his way, or why several officers had to be involved. It was explained to him by another chubby, black officer that three of the guys would be the walking surveillance team. This way, if Rico suspected one of the officers, that particular agent could bail and another would take over. It was the only way 5.0 could outsmart Rico's look-outs.

"We got you covered. Just do what you're told," the black officer said, in a helpful tone. He patted Devon on the shoulder and gave him some privacy.

Devon appreciated the help and headed to an unoccupied corner to secure the wire.

"We all got the same nuts!" Chaney yelled. "Some are pale, some are black, but believe me, they're all the same. Now, if that shit falls out while you're talking to Rico, you're one dead brother. Let somebody help you."

Devon spoke up quickly, "Nah, I'll pass." His tone said that his answer was non-negotiable.

Minutes after Devon's nut sack had been strapped down with the transformer, Don came strutting toward the back of the building. "You ready young blood?" he asked, like he and Devon were old friends.

"What you think, Don King?" he shot back.

"Don't be mad at me. This is the life you chose. Fast cars, movie stars and wires," he joked. It seemed like he'd spritzed his hair so it could stand straight up just before arriving.

Devon wasn't amused at all. He was completely out of focus when Don placed the stack of bills in front of his face. "Ten thousand even," he said, moving the money back and forth.

"Man, these marked bills don't do shit. You haven't figured that out yet?"

"Oh, they will. When we bust his ass, let's just hope for your sake we find enough of them."

"This is a bull-shit stake-out."

"At this point, you're wasting taxpayers money. Let's do this," he said, signaling for Devon to get ready.

Within minutes, Don had laid down the law and the requirements for staying out on the street. He explained that his crew would be watching closely, including the scruffy looking officer dressed as a homeless person. Devon glanced at the officer gathering up his bags, rags, and pushcart, before heading through the gate.

"Wait a minute, son, we leave first," Don said, throwing his arm out in front of Devon.

As Don and his entourage left the area, Devon instantly developed a migraine. If he was caught, today could possibly be his last day on earth. But between the wireless device on the officer's wrist, and the transmitter in the homeless man's cart, he felt sure he'd be safe.

The moment he took his first step out of the gate, it seemed like he was headed to his own funeral. His mind thought back to the reasons why he decided to be a snitch from the start. Devon had always been the type of guy on the streets who would go down fighting. From the outside look-ing in, people who knew him would expect him to suck it up like a man and do his time. It didn't matter if it was life or the chair. He had always preached to Kirk and his other run-ners about loyalty and honor. Yet, here he was, willing to do someone else in, to lessen his time.

Devon thought the worse. *What would people say if this ever got out?* He could hear the streets talking. "That nigga shoulda' opted for the electric chair before he went out like that! What the fuck? If it had been me, I woulda never snitched." Others would say, "I'd just do my time like a man!" Devon knew those comments would be lies, but nonetheless, that's what his boys and enemies would think of him.

Devon stopped in the middle of the sidewalk, just as he had thought of an excuse to make himself feel better. *He did have a good reason, Carlie,* he thought. He attempted to make himself believe she was the reason he would go against the code of the streets. He truly loved Carlie, more than he felt any man could ever love a woman. He punched himself lightly in the side of the head.

"Yes," he mumbled. "She needed me to be out. Kirk was just gonna keep runnin' her crazy with his hoes, and most of all, tryna get at her money." Besides, a part of Devon wanted Ricky to see that he was never that bad of a guy. His intentions were always in the best interest of Carlie. For Devon, his strange logic was enough to convince him to go through with it all.

Six blocks over, he found himself headed to the corner to meet up with Rico. As he walked, the first man on the surveillance team walked a block behind. Devon was told not to look back, but he couldn't resist. The rules were too much for him to follow. Instantly, he crossed the street just to see what would happen. And just like he was told, the officer continued on his path, while another picked up the surveillance behind Devon. *Damn*, he thought, *these mufuckas ain't playin', they on point.*

Devon crossed the street once again as he approached the meeting spot. The playground was packed and noisier than usual. While children ran through the gated grounds, he stood tall with his hands in his pockets, confident on the outside, yet edgy inside. He couldn't help but notice the old homeless man on the nearby sidewalk, who was involved with the sting operation. The man pulled his baseball cap low and closed his dingy overcoat tightly when he spotted Devon looking his way. What Devon didn't know was that he was the officer who held the receiver in one of the bags on his cart.

Devon's attention was diverted when Rico pulled up. His

truck stopped at the corner and he walked toward Devon. As usual, he nodded for Devon to follow him to a more discreet area. Devon knew from Rico's demeanor that something was wrong. Had he been made? Would he try to pop him in broad daylight? He wondered if the officers could still see them as they approached a stairwell, just below a boarded up brownstone.

"What's the problem, playa?" Devon asked, noticing Rico's grimace.

"This drought is fuckin' me up. And everybody is comin' up short."

Devon breathed heavily out of relief. "I pays my bills," he laughed.

"Yeah, you do. But Snake from uptown, Big Cheezie, and that nigga, Kirk, all owe me. Kirk won't even answer my calls."

"I told you 'bout that nigga. You hardheaded. They tell me he just bought a Benz and been splurging big time." Devon lied with a straight face. "As a matter of fact, I heard he used your money to buy a few cars to start his car lot in Jamaica, Queens. You know that nigga ain't gonna pay you," Devon said, in a more serious voice. He was always very persuasive, but even more today as Rico listened carefully.

"Oh, yeah…"

"No doubt. Soon you'll have the whole neighborhood thinkin' you a sucka."

"Nah, I don't think so. I know what to do. So the lot's in Queens?" Rico's look changed drastically for the worse. He didn't wait for an answer. "So, what you got for me?" he asked abruptly.

Devon's heart skipped a beat. *What if the transmitter made a noise*? Uhh…" he stuttered. He wondered if the word *snitch* had been drawn clearly across the top of his forehead. Devon was hesitant about speaking. He stuck his hands deep into his pockets and pulled out a wad of bills. "I need a half key," he said, passing the wad to Rico. He hoped he wouldn't unravel the money. The marked bills had him on edge.

"It's all here?"

"Yeah. You know it."

"Alright, I'll have my man hit you in a few."

Devon panicked. Don's words, *try to get him to serve you, not his boy,* kept repeating in his mind.

"Man, I'm in a hurry. Is there anyway you can snatch it for me now?"

"You know I don't get my hands dirty." Rico rubbed his hands together in a swift motion.

"I know, dog, I'm just in a hurry."

"You know the routine. I don't touch shit!"

From afar, the officers picked up every word. The team watched and listened intently, hoping Devon would keep pushing. They needed as much concrete evidence as possible. Yes, the money would stick, but Rico actually transferring the cocaine from his own hands would seal the deal.

Again, Don's words flashed in Devon's mind. *Make Rico admit what he's selling. It'll help you in the long run.* Devon cleared his throat. "Is this one a'ight, 'cause I got some complaints on that last batch?"

Rico frowned at the strange question. "What you talkin' 'bout? I didn't do nothin', my brother." He already had it planted in his mind that Devon was disturbed. He thought he was untouchable, but to ask a question like that had him puzzled.

Chapter
· · · · · · · · · ·
17

Carlie bit at her nails, waiting for Ricky to call back. She paced the floor, wondering what the outcome would be. She had already called Jewell to book her on the next flight out, but wondered if it was safe. Ricky warned that it might not be a good idea to return to the area. He instructed her to stay put and wait for his call.

As usual, Carlie decided to do things her way. After a few minutes of contemplating, she suddenly started to throw the many gifts and jewels Devon had given her during her short stay into the Gucci garment bag. A quick reality check entered her mind. Everything in her presence was from Devon; the clothes, jewels, even the luggage. She shook her head at how much she'd backtracked in life. In just four short weeks, her life had changed drastically. Devon managed to enter her well-structured life and made her dependent on him once again.

Money wasn't the biggest concern. Carlie could've easily gone to the bank for cash, or had Jewell send her more money. Unconsciously, she was allowing herself to be controlled once again. She thought about the fact that Devon had instructed her to stay in the hotel room because he had to go see his probation officer back in Maryland. The only benefit from him going away was that she'd have time alone to think and do some self-searching.

Just as the last pair of jeans was thrown into the bag, her cell phone rang. Carlie took a quick look at the name and answered on the first ring.

"What did he say?" she asked anxiously.

Ricky breathed heavily. He promised himself before the call that he would control his temper. "Carlie, how can you be so smart, yet so dumb?"

"I don't need to hear this at a time like this."

"No, you do need to hear it. Even the favors I've called in might not be able to help you."

Alarms went off. "What? Tell me!" she screamed.

"There's so much to tell. But first, is there anything you want to tell me?" Ricky wanted her to come clean. He already knew everything, and even though he was angry at Carlie, he was upset at himself.

"Dad, tell me what you found out," she begged. Her voice reached out for help, not an argument.

"China is wide awake. She's doing okay for now." Ricky waited for some type of response, but got none. He expected his daughter to show some concern. "And get this. She's pregnant."

"She is?" Carlie played along. If this was what Ricky was mad about, she could handle that.

Thank God for the plush carpet, because she could've burned holes the way she stepped back and forth across the floor.

"The police have now claimed both of you as official suspects." He spoke slowly, so Carlie could understand his every word. "Detective Travis Peters wants you and Kirk to turn yourselves in." Ricky's voice fumed a bit. "He better turn his ass in before I get to him."

Carlie wasn't sure how much her father knew, but it was clear that Ricky was ready to jump back into his thuggish ways. "He's not important," she responded.

His tone completely changed. "They need that motherfucker for a paternity test! China's three months pregnant."

"So, why do they think its Kirk's? She seems like the type to screw plenty of men."

"When they searched her house, a letter was found. Oddly, it was addressed to you."

"Me?" she asked, in shock.

"Yeah, a friendly little letter, saying she was pregnant and having Kirk's baby." Ricky didn't tell Carlie all the other nasty things China wrote. His inside connection said it was apparent that she intended on harassing Carlie. But, unfortunately, the letter gave Carlie motive to shoot her.

"As soon as we find him, I'm gonna handle that motherfucker!"

Carlie was scared to think about the word *we*. Ricky's background spoke for itself. She prayed he wasn't bringing in any hit men or his boys from the old days. She loved the way her dad turned a complete three-sixty. The law firm was doing well, and he was well-respected. Bringing back his violent ways and activities was borderline scary.

"Do you know that girl even had your damn social security card in her purse? Now that sucka either gave it to her, or she stole it. Either way, he gotta pay for it. Baby girl, we need a plan."

Carlie sat down, ready to listen. She knew getting out of this would take some serious thinking. "Shoot."

"They'll probably issue a warrant if they find out you left town. You need to come back so we can go to the station. I'll have every high paid lawyer in the city ready to walk in that precinct by the time you get here," he bragged. "That's intimidation, baby! Besides, I already talked to Chief Jordan."

Carlie breathed a heavy sigh of relief. "Okay, at least something is working out right."

"Umm, I don't know. The Chief is already upset with us. We scheduled a meeting at a private spot. He didn't say much. But from what I could sense, it seems like if we get Marcus off, then he'll make it hard for you with this situation."

Her voice cracked. "That's framing me."

"It's the name of the game. Everybody does it. No, I don't believe he would set you up to be convicted and locked up, but he'd sic his boys on you a bit harder, just looking for a cause to press some kinda charge."

Carlie's mind began to work as Ricky talked. *No more little Miss Carlie. No more nice shit,* she thought. Her father's comments were going in one ear and right out the other, until he mentioned Kirk again.

"Yeah, the detectives have been playing you both. They threw the bait out and Kirk apparently bit. And I gotta say, I'm sorry," he said, breaking down. His voice trembled a bit. Carlie knew her dad was too strong to actually cry, but he was extremely upset.

"Sorry for what?" she asked.

"For being such a let down. I mean, I'm supposed to protect you. That's what I'm here for."

Carlie could hear the disappointment in his voice. "You do protect me," she responded, trying to make him feel at ease.

"Don't lie. I'm the one who encouraged you to be with Kirk. I knew you didn't love him! But I thought he cared enough about you to keep drama out your life. That motherfucker saw what you went through with Devon!" The louder he got, the more his words started to become jumbled.

Instantly, Carlie got teary eyed. "Dad, calm down. It's okay, it's not your fault. It's me," she cried. Emotions took over, and she tried to settle herself enough to talk. "All my life, I've depended on men. I think about how Devon used to protect me, control me, love me, and then beat me!" She sniffled. "I wanted, no, we wanted him out of my life so bad, that we settled for anybody who appeared to be treating me right on the surface."

"Carlie…"

"No, let me finish," she said, with a stronger voice. "I allowed most of this to happen. The moment I found out about China, he should've been gone. But a part of me wanted to just be in a relationship. And I felt I owed Kirk for sticking with me through the Devon situation."

"You don't owe that motherfucker shit!"

"I realize that now." Carlie took her last sniff. She suddenly spoke with more belief in herself than ever before. "I don't need a no-good ass nigga to make me whole. I should've realized that a long time ago."

Ricky shook his head. He didn't believe *his* daughter was

talking this way. He always wanted her to be stronger, and more in control. Cursing was what he wanted to hear. College was behind her, law school was a success, and her career was further along than most people in their fifties. He only wished she had found a respectable man to treat her right.

Deep inside, he knew Carlie wanted children. She never talked about it much, but she slipped up and commented on having a house full of children a few months ago. But with all of her problems, he could sleep at night not being a grandfather, but he wouldn't rest until his baby girl was out of her mess.

"Dad, what about the case?"

"Oh, don't worry about that. I got it."

"It's my responsibility, and I need to come back and step up to the plate."

"That bastard Willard is out to get you. He keeps making it known that you aren't around. His career has been so horrible, he's trying to make it on this case."

"I'll show him. I'm a Stewart," she said jokingly.

Ricky was thrilled to see her mood change. This is what he wanted. This is what she needed. Carlie was smart and he knew it. For some reason, she always allowed men to cause her to lose her common sense.

He quickly jumped into work mode, updating Carlie on the weak evidence against Marcus Dupree. As he rambled on, Carlie slipped off into a daze. The phone sat low on her ear, as she went into a mode of her own. *Plan mode.*

Ricky always taught her to plan, and now it was time to act. She shook her head at her own thoughts, as if her father wasn't still talking. She decided at that moment to stop being vulnerable, to take a stand and cut dead weight. Her first step would be to get her money back from Kirk, or at least have him answer to fraud charges. She smiled, thinking about Kirk holding her hand in the coffee shop, and helping her sign the loan paperwork.

The question was, how much *get back* was she willing to dish out? Her options were like playing craps. Her first idea was jail time, he deserved getting bent over in the penitentiary? But another part of her wanted him to suffer even more. The thought of him never holding his unborn child made Carlie smile.

"Dad," she called out, interrupting his ranting. "I need you to do me a favor. It's really, really, really, important." Carlie spoke slowly and seriously. "I need you to cover for me. I promise you I know what I'm doing."

"Ah shit! This sounds bad."

"No, it's good. I just need some time. No more being a stupid-ass for me."

"That's good," Ricky said.

"If you've never trusted my judgment before, I need you to now."

"I'll try. What is it?"

"Call the Chief and the detectives. Let them know I'll be coming in to answer all their questions." Carlie grinned. "With all our lawyers, of course. Set it up," she ordered. "But, most importantly, make sure they know I'm out of town."

"Now why would I say that?"

"Because it's important." Her slight frustration was beginning to show. "They need to know I'm not there. Just trust me!"

"I do trust you, but it sounds crazy as hell. They might want to arrest you."

"You can handle that."

"Tell me this. You're not planning on messing with that girl, China. Are you?"

"C'mon now, I'm not that stupid." While Carlie spoke with a clear head, her mind thought another way. The idea had crossed her mind a few times, but she decided against it. China being in the hospital was good enough for her. As long as she didn't start any mess and jeopardize her freedom, she'd forget about everything.

"Alright. The ball is in your court. You just keep in touch."

"I will. One last thing."

Ricky nearly dropped the phone when his daughter's request registered. *Why would she want his number?*

Chapter
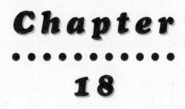
18

Just as Devon slammed the phone down, Don snickered from behind. "What's wrong, young blood? Wifey not too happy 'bout you staying out all night?" He made fun of the man who would get him a promotion, and provoked the other officers to join in. "Be happy we let you use the cell," he added.

Devon shot big Don a dirty look. His worn-out expression showed he hadn't slept all night. Even though his excuse for not sleeping was worrying about Carlie, the others didn't have a choice. The round the clock surveillance was mandatory, as they waited for the infamous call.

Don had managed to convince his boss and an important judge they had enough evidence to make a move on Rico. So, while they waited on the approved paperwork, no one was allowed to leave. Exactly twenty-six hours had passed, and Devon was still in unofficial custody with six funky grown men. He would've given up a thousand dollars just to get a quick shower, or even get a little more space.

The cramped rented room that sat above the convenience store near Devon's workplace was far from comfortable, but worked perfectly for Don. The closeness gave him an opportunity to stare Devon in his face and work the nerves of everyone. The officers were already pissed when they learned that Don wanted to have Devon try to get more evidence one last time. No one saw the need. It was obvious there was enough proof to arrest Rico, even without him actually touching the cocaine.

Don walked the room energetically with his chest extended, while some officers dozed off. The cop who played the part of the homeless man was really taking his role seriously. His long body lay stretched out in the far corner with bags surrounding him, like a homeless man on the street. Even though he slept, his hand remained clutched on his case, ready for action.

Devon watched everyone closely, still disbelieving that he was in a room with a bunch of cops and walkie-talkies. Someone walking in would've surely sworn they were all buddies. He held his head low, and tried to think positive. If all went well, he'd get Rico to say, or do one more thing to top the case. Then Rico would be locked up, and he would be an official *snitch*.

Devon wished he'd told Carlie the truth. Telling her lies when she needed him most didn't sit well with him. And being away from her angered him even more. *What if Kirk was laid up with his woman? What if she decided to go back to Massachusetts?* He thought about the way she acted when he called her phone a moment ago. Although pleasant, she basically rushed him off the line. *The spa*, he thought. *Why would she want to go to a spa at a time like this?* He tried to convince her to wait until he returned, but she insisted it would relieve some stress.

Devon leaned back in the wobbly chair and closed his eyes for a brief moment, hoping the call would come soon.

* * *

Carlie grinned, thinking about how Ricky had come through for her. Not only did he give her the phone number she requested, he made the call first to set some ground rules. After all, she was his baby girl, and he had dealt with these people before.

As Carlie strutted to meet the mystery man, she reviewed her plan one last time. In a strange way, she was scared, but had faith everything would work out. Kirk had done too much, it was almost as if he was trying to destroy her. This was becoming too frequent with the men she dealt with. Carlie wasn't taking any chances with letting him get away without a war mark. She needed to teach him a lesson.

With so many pieces to the overall mission on the table, she had to decide where to start. Filing charges for forgery was one job. Handling the police situation back in Massachusetts was another. And telling Rico a few lies about Kirk was at the top of the list. With three strikes, she knew he'd be out. Something was bound to work.

When Carlie checked her watch, she panicked. Her meeting was scheduled for 3 p.m., and she was just arriving at the bank. Inside, she quickly searched for someone who could help get her in and get out. She prayed that since no one knew her personally at the bank, there wouldn't be a problem withdrawing that kind of money. She signed the notepad lying on the mantle, and took a seat on the couch waiting for a representative to call her name.

A thin, white girl with a frizzy ponytail walked her way. "Hi, can I help you?" she asked Carlie.

"Sure, I'd like to make a withdrawal. This isn't my home branch, so I figured you could help."

"Ohhhhh," she sung, wondering why Carlie was bothering her instead of going to see a teller. "They could've helped you over there." She pointed to the line at the window.

Carlie giggled. "You don't understand. I need to withdraw a substantial amount of money."

"Oh," the woman responded, with her neck popped back. "Well, I'd love to help you. Follow me."

As soon as Carlie sat down at the desk, she smiled, and pulled out her license and account number. She thought, *as soon as I get the money, and put it in the appropriate hands, part one of my plan will be done.*

"How much would you like?" the woman asked, breaking Carlie's trance.

As soon as Carlie answered, the woman's face turned slightly pale. At first, she just knew that when she checked the account, Carlie's request would exceed the balance. But the numbers don't lie. Carlie indeed had enough in the account to cover the request and much more.

Soon, her top-secret plan would be into phase two. As she left the bank, her purse was loaded with crisp hundreds. The meeting place had already been arranged, and the mystery man knew exactly how long he had to make everything work.

Carlie hopped in a cab and headed to the Magic Theater. Within minutes she arrived, bought a ticket, and entered the building. In the dimly lit theater, she searched for the third row from the top. Her eyes squinted as she tried to catch a quick glance at the few figures nearby. Although she didn't know what her man looked like, she figured he'd be big and well-dressed. After all, he had connections in big places. Carlie remembered the wild stories Ricky had told her in the past about him. And if Ricky was able to brag about him, then he was definitely someone who would handle things correctly.

Carlie started to sweat when she noticed most of the rows were empty. But suddenly she noticed a slim guy sitting stiffly in the third row of the center aisle. He wore a bulky sweatshirt, and a baseball cap pulled just above his eyes. He didn't look like the guy she expected to meet, but his position was perfect. She thought back to their initial phone conversation. She remembered him saying to come in and sit directly behind him.

Instantly, she backed up and found a discreet spot near the back. Standing still, she whipped the money from her purse and placed it into the brown envelope as instructed. Then, she slipped the note with the specific instructions into the bag. For Carlie, the top-secret plan was becoming a bit spooky.

As soon as the package was ready, she headed down the aisle and scooted through the seats. The closer she got to the man, she thought he'd turn around to make eye contact. He never did.

So, in perfect position, she sat and waited. He had warned not to pass the package until his hand lifted in the air, silently requesting it. The average person would've been scared to death, just said fuck it, and left. But Carlie knew she had to see the deal through. Ricky made it clear before she started to make sure she really wanted to get back at Kirk. And she did.

Every time a move was made, she looked for a sign that his hand was in the air. Impatiently, she twitched in the seat, hoping he'd look back. Minutes passed, and Carlie grew more impatient. Just as soon as she decided to leave, his hand appeared in the air. Carlie slapped the brown envelope into his palms and sat back. She almost forgot the agreement was to wait until he left first. With part two under her belt, she grinned at the thought of the next step.

Over the next hour, headed to the heart of Harlem, Carlie pumped herself up with courage. She had no idea what Rico actually looked like, but trusted that her paid connection set her up with the right guy. When the cab driver let her out two streets from the block, she stood like a lost puppy. Even though her mind played tricks, and fear bubbled up in her system, the job had to be done.

When she approached Rico, he was standing in the middle of the sidewalk. Slightly to his left, there was a crowd of people, some who were watching Carlie with an evil eye. A few policemen on the block carried nightsticks, but no guns. She thought, *if something goes down, I don't know who's gonna help me.*

"What's up? I'm Carlie," she said faintly. "I guess you're wondering why I'm here?"

Rico didn't wonder. He knew she was there to be a cut-throat. He had dealt with plenty of conniving women, and figured Carlie wanted revenge on Kirk.

"I know why you're here. Believe me, if I didn't, you wouldn't have this chance."

Carlie's intent was to make it seem like she was doing him

a favor. "Be glad I'm helping you out," she smirked.

Rico wasn't into making new friends, but in her case, a sexy new friend was good. *She could be potentially poisonous,* he thought. *But damn, one night with her might be worth it.* His reaction to Carlie was strange. He'd never met a beautiful woman that he was mesmerized by. Her presence had him flustered. He knew she was there to take care of business, but it was something about her that had him sprung.

"I'm trying to keep you outta deep shit." She tried her best to be hip.

"Oh, you are," he remarked, as he looked her up and down.

As she continued to talk, he finally understood why Kirk and Devon fought over her. She was well worth it, from top to bottom. Hell, she was the type of woman who could juggle ten boyfriends at the same time. He imagined spoiling her aboard his 45-foot boat.

"Look, do you wanna know what Kirk has planned for you?"

"Why should I believe you?" he asked, looking directly at the black knitted shirt that fit tightly across her breast.

"Because I have nothing to gain. But I thought you should know."

"Did Devon set all this up? That nigga wants to get back at Kirk bad."

"Did Devon contact you?" she asked sarcastically.

"No, but he could've set up the meetin' just like you did."

Carlie started to worry. Convincing Rico wasn't as easy as she'd thought. She'd have to take drastic measures, if necessary. "Look, do you wanna know or not? It would be a shame for a cutie like you to go to jail," she said, in a sexy-like manner.

Rico liked her change in character. He wanted her from the start, and the flirtatious body language she was giving off, was turning him on.

"So, what you got for me?"

"Kirk, got it in for you," she blurted out. "I'd hate to see that happen to a fine man like you." When her finger slid across the bottom of Rico's lip, he instantly got a hard-on. He tried hard to keep his focus on what Carlie was saying. "I heard him talking to a few people about robbing you."

"What the fuck? Who was he talkin' to?"

"I have no idea. I do know that he's jealous of you." She smiled. "He talks about how much money you making and how you the man. I bet he didn't even pay you the money he owes?"

That was all Rico needed to hear. Kirk hadn't paid him, and for Carlie to know it, meant she was telling the truth. He got up close in Carlie's face. The scent of her body had his thoughts going ballistic.

"Why you all of a sudden interested in what happens to me?"

"Cause he hurt me badly, and I'd hate to see him do the same to you. Besides, I wanna pay him back. You know, this is my revenge."

"You must not care what happens to him by tellin' me some shit like this. Cause when my boys go after him, he may not come back to you in one piece."

"I'm done with him."

"Does that mean you're ready for me?"

"Of course," Carlie lied. "It's time for a real man."

Carlie's goal was to try and woo Rico as much as she

could. She needed him to believe her. But when Rico reached out and ran his fingers through her hair, she was shocked. Yes, she wanted him to fall for her, but damn. She looked away, not realizing he'd already caught her blushing. So he went in for the kill.

"Call me on my personal number this evenin'. I'll take care of Kirk. Girl, you too pretty, I gotta look out for you. You hear me?"

Carlie shook her head, dying for him to let go. Instead, he pulled her close and kissed her in the middle of the street. The minute she tasted his kiss, she felt trashy. Here she was mixing saliva with a short Columbian motherfucker she hardly knew, *all to get back at Kirk.*

At that same moment, across the street the homeless man and another member of Don's surveillance team motioned for Devon to wait at the corner until the unidentified woman left the scene. Frustrated, Devon didn't want to wait. He wanted to ignore the boss man's signal. He'd already been on lockdown with the undercovers for way too long. So what if Rico was with a woman, all he wanted was to record one last conversation, so he could go back to his woman.

Just as Rico released Carlie, he backed away wearing a big grin. "I'll be waitin' for the call," he ended, clutching at his crouch.

At the same time, Devon spotted Carlie and his eyes damn near popped out of his head. The officers could tell from his expression that something was wrong, and attempted to intercede. As Devon sprinted into the middle of the street, headed in Carlie's direction, he turned to see Rico getting back in the SUV. All kinds of violent thoughts entered his head. He didn't know whether to go after Carlie first and beat the shit out of her, or steal somebody's gun and snatch Rico out of his truck.

Devon behaved like a wild maniac. He cracked his knuckles in a panic and walked with a killer swagger. Messing up the entire stake-out wasn't a concern to him, so when the officer dressed as the homeless guy gave him the eye, he ignored his gesture. He thought, *so what if Rico saw anythin' go down.*

If Carlie had seen the veins popping from Devon's head, she would've known he was coming for her. Instead, she stood halfway in the street hailing a cab, like she had conquered her task. Five yards away, Devon ran faster! He was almost there! Just as the cab pulled up, the undercover appeared and stood in front of it.

As Carlie pulled off, he spoke clearly to Devon. "Don't mess this up. Somebody from Rico's camp could be watching. Turn around and go back to your location. Don't lose your head, we're almost there."

The look on Devon's face showed he was done with cooperating.

He turned around slowly as Carlie's cab disappeared down the avenue.

Chapter
• • • • • • • • • • •
19

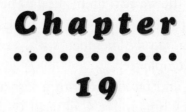

Kirk's presence in the hospital had the entire nursing station buzzing. It was a blessing that China hadn't lost her baby in the shooting, and a double blessing that the baby survived while she was in her comatose state. Now, with China fifteen weeks pregnant, the nurses at Boston Memorial Hospital were calling her baby the miracle baby.

So, it was no surprise when Kirk came bursting in the ward, saying he was China's man. He was thrown questions like a fast-ball on a baseball field. "Didn't somebody tell you she gets visits from five to six?" a skinny nurse said. "Who are you? We've never seen you."

"And guess what? I never seen you either," he said sarcastically.

"She's not taking any visitors at the moment," a sassy, heavy-set nurse interrupted.

"I'm her man, she would want me here," Kirk shot back, walking the halls reading the small nameplate on each door.

"Well, where the hell you been all this time?" the nurse

asked. China had been awake for over a week, and no phone calls from Kirk had come in, no flowers, nothing.

Kirk looked back as he headed down the hall. He was shocked to see the woman on his heels. She was nearly three-hundred pounds, and stood with her hands on her hips. She behaved like a family member with a vested interest in China, not an employee.

He turned and faced her with a kiss-my-ass expression. "I'm gonna see China today. Call security, do what you gotta do," he said, noticing China's name above the door in front of him. "She'll tell you, I'm staying."

It was obvious Kirk still had plenty of confidence in the way China felt about him. The moment he laid eyes on her, he couldn't believe it was her. Although bandages draped her face, and were wrapped in three different directions across her head, she sat in bed, rubbing her stomach with a smile. Kirk had rarely seen her smile before. There was no cluttered make-up like she normally wore. No nasty-mouth language, just happy to be alive and pregnant.

China smiled long enough for the guard dog to walk away when Kirk entered the room. Then the smile turned into a bit of a frown. Even though she was happy to see him, she wondered where he'd been. For six days and six nights, while in a deep sleep, she heard officers coming in, and doctors going out, but nothing from Kirk.

She looked him over, noticing his freshly starched jeans and new leather jacket. He looked like a million bucks, like he'd come into some real money. She wondered what was really going on and decided to ask. His response was romantic and a straight lie, but just what China needed to hear.

"Baby, I've been in and out of town setting up shop so we

can have a good life. What, you never believed what I told you I was doing for us?"

"Umh...hmm," she responded. China had her doubts about what she was hearing, but it damn sure sounded good. "So, why you haven't been to see me?"

"Shit, I was scared to come around because it seemed like the cops were trying some tricky shit. Like they wanna put some blame on me for you getting shot."

"Ahh, hell nah! I told'em that puta, Carlie, shot me dead and center. They keep comin' back with extra shit. I think somebody is feedin' them nonsense."

"I'm still tryna understand how you broke into Carlie's house, and now I'm a suspect. It doesn't make sense." Kirk looked at China for answers. His next statement put China on the spot. "The police found a letter that you wrote to Carlie."

China looked away.

"Why'd you write Carlie a letter saying that you was pregnant, instead of just telling me? You know I'm gonna be there for my child."

At first she shrugged her shoulders as she considered being ignorant as usual. Then, her attitude changed. "I know it was a stupid move, that's why I never mailed it. The letter wasn't nothin' to get all hyper about. That detective is just looking for trouble."

"No doubt. But you gave him something to get hyper about."

China quickly changed the subject when she saw the look in Kirk's eyes. "Well, they've lightened up a bit now that I'm gonna make it. The detectives told me it would've been a murder case if I'd died. So be thankful, nigga!"

"You stole my key, didn't you?" He paused. China didn't respond. "What would make you break into her house? You could've been killed, or killed her!"

China snapped for the first time since his visit. "Be glad I didn't tell the police what they wanna hear. I could've easily told them the second shot was meant to take my ass out." She rolled her eyes toward Kirk, then changed her demeanor as if she had two personalities. "My baby is all I need."

"You right, nothing else matters right now." Kirk leaned in toward her bed, grabbing at each finger. "This finger won't be naked for long," he said, referring to the one he'd place an engagement ring on.

Once again, China wasn't sure what to believe. Kirk seemed sincere, but he'd seemed sincere a few times in the past too. What she didn't know was that Kirk was devastated at how Carlie had dissed him for Devon.

He thought back to how he saved her from Devon years ago, moved with her all the way to Massachusetts, and now this. He'd even heard on the street that Carlie and Devon were out to get him. Going back to Carlie was a no-no. It was all about he and China from here on out.

"So, tell me about our baby," he said.

China rubbed her belly once again. It was so small, you could barely tell she was pregnant. "I'm three months," she bragged.

Kirk calculated with speed. He wanted to make sure it was his. Although he was scheduled for a paternity test at the request of Detective Travis Peters, he wanted to know for himself first. His mind scrolled, searching for the last time they'd had unprotected sex. *Not often*, he thought.

But then it hit him. There was a time about three to four

months ago where he went bare-back.

"It's yours," China barked, breaking Kirk's trance.

"Why would you say something like that?" he asked, laughing.

"I know how you think." China thought maybe it was a good idea to tell Kirk about her turkey injector stunt. Then she quickly changed her mind. There was no need in telling him anything. She had become pregnant without it, and it didn't even matter. What mattered was her getting out of the hospital and she and Kirk starting their new family.

"How you know how I think?" he asked jokingly. "Listen up, whatever problems we had in the past, whatever confusion with me, you and Carlie, that's over." He grabbed China's hand once more. "I promise you, no more of that."

"I wanna believe yo ass. But you make it hard for a bitch. So, what if Carlie wants you back?" she asked bluntly.

Shocked, Kirk thought about the question. "I dumped her!" He pointed at himself with a tint of embarrassment on his face. "I decided to let it go. She wasn't true to me, and I was never true to her." He smiled.

"So, it's really over?"

"No doubt."

China wanted to leap from the bed, and wrap her arms and legs around Kirk like a horny octopus. She was happier inside than she'd ever been, but didn't want to seem overly-excited. A small part of her didn't believe he was truly over Carlie.

"Kirk, it's not just me and you anymore," she stated, giving him the evil eye. This time she grabbed at his hand. "They're three of us." She placed his hand on top of her belly, and moved it slowly in a circular motion.

No one would've predicted such a happy moment for Kirk and China. It was a relationship expected to fail. But things were all of a sudden turning in the right direction for them. As Kirk said his goodbyes, and headed toward the door, his favorite nurse passed by.

"Hey, take good care of my woman," he called out. A pair of rolling eyes caught his stare.

"We will, and we hope to see you more often," she said, with her lip twisted up.

For the first time in Kirk's life, he thought he was doing the right thing, and it felt good. No one had ever needed him the way China did. As a younger boy, he was number nine of twelve children, and just that, *a number.* As he got older, he pretty much broke away from his dysfunctional family and made his own way in life. Shortly thereafter, there was Devon by his side. The two were boys for over nine years until Devon went to jail. Just enough time for him to betray his boy and steal Carlie.

Just when he thought having Carlie was enough and would fulfill his life, he betrayed her too. The sneakiness, being conniving, the cheating, it was all to satisfy himself. Never mind what Carlie had suffered, it made Kirk happy.

As he walked, he realized it was time to bring joy to someone else's life. Maybe that's what he'd been missing all these years. With China and the new baby, he'd have an opportunity to give his baby something he never had, *a real family.* He grinned and pressed the up button in front of the parking elevators.

As soon as he exited the elevator into the dimly lit garage, he reached into his pockets for the small parking ticket to exit the facility. He was pissed for not getting his ticket stamped before leaving. Parking was eight dollars an hour, and he'd been there over two hours.

As he paused, thinking about going back, a shadow was noticed from out the side of his eye. He dropped all thoughts about going back, dug deeper for the ticket, and reached for his keys at the same time. Kirk thought about the stack of hundreds in his pocket. There was probably close to two-thousand dollars, and he'd definitely put up a fight if he had to. He'd never heard any bad stories about robberies at the hospital, but he was starting to have creepy thoughts.

His pace quickened, as he looked for his ride. When he spotted the ramp next to aisle C, an isolated car passed and made him feel slightly better. Knowing it was close to midnight, he didn't expect to see any people going to their cars. But the shadow he'd seen must've come from the person leaving.

"Aisle B," he said aloud, reminding himself where the car was parked. As he continued to search for the car, a ghost-like feeling came over him. Not a sole was in sight, but he felt the presence of someone.

Kirk spotted the car in the middle of the aisle, and walked swiftly, with key in hand. Out of nowhere a large shadow appeared again, causing him to move even faster. For the first time, he heard footsteps. Slow footsteps. He panicked, just as he reached the car. Nervously, he fought with the key and door handle, trying to get in.

Just as he looked back over his shoulder, a huge figure dressed in all black, holding a black object stood without fear. The gunman waited until Kirk took off running before he blasted. The significance was important. Revenge was the message. When the first shot hit him in the back, Kirk knew why his assailant didn't shoot him in the face.

Even though the pain fired straight through his body, he managed to tread slowly with a limp. The next two shots were fired in rapid succession, knocking him to the ground. Kirk fell face up, able to see the attacker clearly moving closer in his direction. He spent the next few seconds trying to get a good description of the assailant with average height. He figured if he lived, he'd be able to give some sort of description.

The attempted killer appeared to be shaped like a man, looking as if he was headed on a ski trip or doing a drive-by. Everything was black, from the knitted hat to the black facemask. The thuggish way he dressed in his heavy down coat, with black jeans beneath; if any witnesses were nearby, they would know something was going down.

Kirk had done a lot of treacherous things in life, and to people who'd always done right by him. Any number of people could want him dead, or someone could just need a little money. Just as he squirmed, trying to reach his pocket to pull out a wad of money, a large foot pressed his hand to the ground. The throbbing sensation felt like the wheels of a train grinding on a track. But the mixed pain from his gunshot wounds, and his broken fingers were so unbearable, he could barely scream.

The intent was clear as the assailant lifted one foot over Kirk's motionless body and stood directly above him. The only opening in the face- mask showed off his evil-looking eyes. They stared Kirk down with a silent, evil warning that said, *don't say a fuckin' word.* Kirk watched him turn to search the scene, just before he made his next move. He thought about trying to get away, but decided against it, as the blood seeped from his back out into the open where he could see it.

The gunman noticed the thick, red blood too. At the sight of it, he dove his hands deep into Kirk's pocket and yanked out the bills. Just when Kirk thought, *maybe this was a robbery?* The next few moves happened in slow motion.

Suddenly, the gunman backed slightly away from Kirk's body, like he was ready to leave. *Maybe he heard someone coming,* Kirk thought. His body wouldn't even allow him to get happy. As his eyes rolled up in the back of his head, the loss of blood had him hallucinating. The more his vision faded away, the more it seemed like the shooter was leaving. Two seconds later, a shot was fired. On target, the bullet entered the rear of Kirk's side, and severed his spinal cord. Perfect hit! That fourth and final shot did the trick and sealed the deal.

The sound of oncoming tires sent the shooter running. A woman pulling up the ramp in a Cadillac drove like a maniac. Not coming to help, but trying her best to get away. She'd heard the shot and managed to get a glimpse of the shooter. Scared for her life, she backed up going 70 miles per hour searching for help, and leaving Kirk to fend for himself.

His body squirmed on the cold concrete. While he gasped for air, the garage spun in a fast circle. With no help on the way, he closed his eyes and slumped over.

Chapter
•••••••••
20

Devon entered the room, pumped up and with a fake-ass smile. Moments before, he stood in the hallway and wiped the sweat from his body. Between running after Carlie and his anxiety, he was soaked. He thought about the techniques learned when he was in anger management, and breathed a few times when he looked at Carlie. It nearly killed him to be nice. He'd already realized that the foolish idea of running off a federal case to chase Carlie was going to have him in a lot of trouble, but Carlie had to pay.

He grinned wickedly when she asked what was in the bag, when he walked pass. Maybe she thought there was something in there for her. He wanted to tell her the truth. He wanted to come out and say, *fuckin' duct tape, bitch. So I can tape your ass up and put a bullet through your head.* Instead, he smiled, but Carlie could sense a bit of uneasiness.

She tried to lighten the mood by asking Devon if he'd eaten. Before he could respond, she plopped down on the side of the bed, reaching for the phone. Devon's strong hand pounced on top of hers.

"Who you callin'?"

"Room service," she responded with sarcasm. She wondered about his strange behavior.

"We not eatin' right now," he said, still gripping her hand forcefully. Devon cringed at the short, skimpy, white velour tunic she wore. It reminded him of a freaky Frederick's of Hollywood outfit, and also gave him visions of Rico's hand planted firmly on Carlie's exposed butt cheeks.

He fumed! Within moments, she was flat on her back, and Devon sat straddling the mid-section of her body. She could feel his hardness getting harder by the minute. Devon grinded a bit, but his facial expression remained grim.

For Carlie, it felt good, but his weirdness kept her from joining in his freaky movements. *He was handsome, yet a crazy man*, she thought. Her mind drifted to the sexual fun they'd had a few days ago. Even though Carlie hadn't expected to have sex with Devon again before leaving, she was being sucked in. He grinded harder and her body begged for it.

Abruptly, he asked, "How was the spa today?"

"The best," she answered, without missing a beat.

"Your skin feels so smooth," he said, rubbing her arms roughly. "What did you get?"

Carlie paused momentarily. "Ah…a package deal. A lil' bit of this and lil' bit of that."

Devon grew increasingly agitated, watching Carlie lie. He behaved strangely as he looked into her eyes. He continued to rub her body as his stroke became increasingly rougher.

Carlie couldn't put a finger on it, but he didn't really want to make love. "Where'd you go today?" he asked.

"Devon, I already told you."

"You not hidin' nothin', are you?"

"Why...why would I do that?" she stuttered. Carlie knew she was caught. Devon had either followed her or had her followed. That was his pattern. She wanted to smack herself for forgetting how he used to watch her closely.

Devon gripped the back of her neck and pressed her head toward the phone. "Pick it up," he said.

Carlie looked confused. "For what, who you want me to call?"

"Call the spa, bitch!" he shouted.

"For what, Devon? Plus, I don't know the number," she answered, hoping he'd loosen his grip just a bit.

"The front desk," he said, gritting his teeth. "The front desk will connect you. Now call!"

Carlie pressed the button for the front desk. All along, she wondered how things would go down. She prayed there wouldn't be an answer at the spa, because she knew Devon was gonna whip her ass good.

"Yes, can you connect me..."

"Hang up!" Devon yelled. "We ain't gon' sit here and play fuckin' games. You know your lyin' ass wasn't there! I gotta lil' secret," he said, releasing her neck and pressing her back against the headboard. "I was there." The first bang upside the head with the phone made Carlie realize he knew something.

"What are you talking about?" she asked, as her chest pounded. "Where? When?"

"Bitch, I didn't get out on a technicality. I got out with a job to do. I still got a prison number attached to my name."

Carlie was scared and confused, but refused to cry. She

watched the anger in Devon's eyes, as he paused like he was ready to whip out his gun and blow her brains out.

"What is… ?"

"Don't fuckin' say nothin'. I'm doin' the mufuckin' talkin'. I'm out there on the block with the possibility of gettin' my ass blasted, and my girl is talkin' to the nigga that I gotta set up!"

Carlie's expression showed she was still confused. One thing was for sure. She was caught!

"I'm a snitch! Have you gotten so prissy you don't know what's goin' on?" His hate-filled eyes said, if she answered the wrong way, she would be done. "I was out there with a team of undercovers, and all because of your ass, I'm here! They probably gettin' my papers ready to send my ass back to jail now!" Suddenly, the sound of Devon's fist hitting Carlie's face was a reality check for her. Yes, the old Devon was back.

"I had it good. All I had to do was set Rico up, and I was home free. Nobody knew. Yo smart-ass father didn't even know. He knows all the big shots, got all the connects and that mufucka didn't know."

"Nobody still don't have to know. Devon, it's not what you think."

"Shut the fuck up! I was out on the streets with the undercovers and saw you with my own eyes. That lil' mufucka kissed you! And I ran from my damn case, fuckin' with you. And yo ass ain't even worth it. Fuckin' tramp! Of all people, you gon' fuck with my man!"

"No…"

She was hit again, and blood flew from her mouth. She must've had a strong set of teeth to withstand such a powerful punch. As her face dropped to the side, he continued to yell.

"I been fucked…!" Devon stopped in mid-sentence as her body shivered. Chill bumps covered her arms, but no sympathy was coming from Devon. This time it was more serious than in the past. It was his drug connect. "I been fucked many times by hatin'-ass niggas on the street, and even money hungry tramps. But you!" He looked at her with deadly fire in his eyes. "Never this. You tryna fuck my boy? The nigga I get my hustle on with?"

"Devon, it's not like that!" she yelled out. She wanted to get a feel of her sore jaw, but knew Devon would react.

"Shhhhh," he said, placing his finger over her lips. "How the fuck I'ma show my face on the streets without a nigga laughin' at me?"

Carlie clutched the sheets, expecting his blow. As soon as she shut her eyelids, she could feel Devon picking her up like a rag doll. He pressed her upper body against the bedpost. "Lyin' whore! I'ma ask you one last time." His grip tightened. "What the fuck was you doin' with Rico today?"

"I was trying to get him to go after Kirk and…" She screamed out loud after feeling the punch, which seemed to come with the force of ten men.

"You think I believe that bull-shit. You was tongue kissing my man in the middle of the street!"

"But…"

"Shut the fuck up!" She was hit with another heavy stroke.

Carlie whimpered, but didn't drop one tear. Knowing she had survived the past, made her fearless. Yes, it hurt like hell, but she was ready to accept whatever happened.

"I should beat your fuckin' face with my bare fist. Go put

on a skimpy outfit and flag down a vehicle. Let's go." Carlie couldn't figure out if he was serious.

"Change my clothes?" she mumbled.

Devon reached down on the side of the bed and dug into his bag, with half his weight leaning off the bed. Carlie never did figure out what was in the bag, but scrambled to wiggle away from his hold when she saw him sit up with the huge grey roll of duct tape.

"This is gonna hurt me more than it hurts you. Nothin' else needs to be said. Sit back and take it like a woman," he said, in crazy tone.

Carlie managed to get a few screams out for help before the tape was strapped tightly across her mouth. But for every scream, she would pay. As her head bobbed back and forth like a pinned down mental patient, Devon went to work. Every chance she got, she'd use her hands to shield the beating, but it wasn't helping too much.

Devon retaliated. Her hands being in the way made him even angrier. The next thing Carlie knew, Devon's fist came down like a hammer and smashed her finger into the side of the bed, trying his best break it off. The bleeding wasn't enough for him to stop, the muffled hollering wasn't enough either. He banged and banged until his point was clear.

Devon took Carlie's kicks and movements with her legs as a sign of disobedience and struck at her body even harder. Only now, her nose seemed to be the main target. Repeatedly, he punched at her tiny nose, dead set on breaking it. Before long, Carlie's bruised face was a mixture of a reddish and purple combination, sure to turn black within hours. With her head spinning, Carlie lay back, giving into her hell-bound situation. There was no escaping Devon.

Fifteen minutes had gone by, and the strength of Devon's strokes became weak. Besides fighting like he was in the ring without non-stop rounds, he was tired from the rough night before. As he looked down at Carlie, he noticed her starry-eyed look. As far as he was concerned, she'd been taught her first lesson.

The next step was to march her down near Rico's spot and have her face them both. If Rico lied too, he'd blast him on the spot. He pushed at Carlie's shoulder to wake her up.

"Girl, let's get you cleaned up," he said.

Carlie's body lay stiff. Devon pushed her again, and moved in closer to listen to her chest. Yeah, she was still alive. *A murder beef is all I need*, he thought.

Instantly, he decided to rush to the bathroom for a towel to clean some of the blood from her face, and get some water from the faucet. *Maybe a drink will bring some life to her.*

Just as he made it to the bathroom, and the sound of the running water was heard, Carlie's eyes opened fast. Along with the numb feeling inside, there was a desire to try and make it out. She didn't truly believe Devon would kill her, but the beating was just the beginning to constant torture. With no time to grab a thing, her mind raced. No clothes, no shoes and no purse! *Fuck it*, she thought.

Quickly, she sprinted from the bed, ignoring the throbbing pain. She moved like an Olympic medalist running the 400-yard dash. With the door in sight, she could feel Devon's heavy wrath two steps behind her.

Three inches from the knob, the sound of the fall startled them both. Carlie looked back to see Devon face down on the floor. *Nothing but the Lord.* She turned the lock, twisted the knob, and jetted down the hall like a determined escapee.

Barefoot, with a bloody velour tunic on, she passed an elderly couple, who froze at the sight of her. She thought about begging them for help, but knew Devon would beat them too, if necessary.

The way she ran toward the elevator looked like Tina Turner running from Ike. Carlie knew the only way she'd make it was the elevator or the stairs. Quickly, she contemplated both and pressed the down button on the elevator. Just as she snatched her finger back, Devon was once again sprinting like a racehorse. Carlie knew she'd surely die this time if she didn't get away. As she turned to race toward the staircase, the elevator doors opened. The younger detective, alongside Big Don, snatched her into his arms.

"Whoooaaa, lil' lady. We got you!"

As soon as Carlie heard the whisper, "It's okay, I'm a cop," she closed her eyes. She believed the handsome young detective, with the gentle touch, would keep her safe. Her head vibrated from the various sounds heard next.

Within seconds, the largest officer had tackled Devon and pinned his hands behind his back, while the other officers were scattered about the floor. Devon received a miniature version of the beating he'd given Carlie.

In between the punches, Don screamed, "Stupid motherfucker, we the police! Don't you think we had enough sense to follow you?"

Devon didn't respond. He took his punches like he was some type of terminator. With every punch, his eyes remained on Carlie.

"You fucked yourself, son! And you gon' still help us get Rico."

Don thought about the way Devon was getting whipped.

He knew it would be a few days before Devon's bruises would heal enough to meet up with Rico. But he made it clear to Devon that he was going to do his part in bringing down Rico, and then he was secretly planning on telling Rico about Devon being a snitch shortly thereafter.

The sound of the handcuffs made Carlie smile. As far as she was concerned, that was it for her and Devon. Forever!

Chapter
• • • • • • • • • •
21

When China saw Detective Travis Peters enter the room, she'd just about had enough. She wanted to be a smart-ass and tell him it wasn't a good look to wear so many damn African chains. She felt like he was coming to work some voodoo on her and her unborn child. Her hands went up in the air and her mouth ignited, going a mile a minute.

"It's over now. I lived! I'm okay. Leave my man the fuck alone!"

"Ma'am, we didn't come to get you upset. We know Kirk was just here to see you." The look on Peter's face said there was some sort of trouble.

"Yes, he was here." China sat straight up, and propped the pillow behind her. "I wanted him here." She glanced over at the heavy-set nurse, wondering if she had called the police on Kirk. *Petty bitch*, she thought. *Here I am tryin' to turn over a new leaf, start actin' life a mother, and she takin' me back to my old character all ready.*

The sad look on the nurse's face sent a reality check up

her spine. Something else was deeply wrong. "What is it?" she asked, with a frantic look in her eyes.

"Kirk was shot tonight."

"Shot? Where? When?" She gripped her stomach, hoping it wasn't deadly. "Is he dead?" She looked around the room for anyone who would answer.

Travis looked downward, and her trusty nurse moved in for support.

"Is he fuckin' dead? Somebody answer me!" she screamed.

The nurse caressed her shoulders, as if she'd known her for years. "He's not dead, baby," she answered quickly. "But he is in critical condition."

China cried out loudly, "Whyyyyyyyy!" Her screams were heard throughout the unit. "Somebody is out to get me, I just know they are!"

"Why would somebody want to get you?" Travis moved in, looking for a clue.

"Look at what's happenin'! I'm all fucked up! Kirk's shot up! What? It'll be my baby next!"

"Noooooo," he assured. "Your baby will be fine." Travis shot the nurse an unpleasant look. "We'll take it from here," he grinned, with a fast show of his dimple. His eyes darted toward the door, signaling her to leave. "We just have a few questions for the lady, then we'll be done."

"Awwww, my God, awwww, my God!" China chanted. She screamed even louder once the nurse disappeared.

The covers twitched in and out between her thighs, and her hands covered her bandaged cheeks. The thought of losing Kirk had her up in arms. "Where is he?" she asked. "I need to see him!"

"You can't. He's in surgery. We were hoping you could tell

us something that would help us figure out how or why this happened?"

"What the fuck would I know?" She threw the pillow from the bed in a rage. "Is he here? In this hospital?" China threw one leg over the bed, attempting to scoot her way to the edge.

"Yes, he's here, but understand, you can't see him now. It's life or death for him right now. You don't want that on your conscience, do you?" Peters asked firmly. "The doctors need to work their magic. Alone," he ended, as if he didn't want to hear any more about it.

China knew there was nothing she could do in the operating room, but felt like she needed to be nearby. She calmed down and sat back to listen further.

"When he was here, did he say anything? Was anybody after him?"

China shot Peters another nasty look, but this time, she had an idea. She wondered why nothing ever worked out right for her in life. She never had any good memories to share, never had a respectable job, a fun loving family, or even a man to call her own.

She remembered having to bang on the door of the only man who had openly said he loved her. Inside, he slept with another woman, and refused to let her in. Humiliating her wasn't the worst crime. After hours of ranting and raving, he eventually called the cops on China. She cried at the thought of him doing that, thinking of how she'd given him her all. She was handcuffed for looting and harassment, and hauled off to jail, while he watched from the window. Even though Kirk's shit stunk, he was the best thing that ever happened to her. And now, he was near death.

"Nooooooo!" she wailed once again, before switching her thoughts. China was well on her way to becoming a mental patient.

Her thoughts turned to Carlie. From what she knew, she had it all. She grew up sheltered by her father. Rich father at that, and never had a worry in the world. She got angrier at the thought of Carlie having men fighting over her. *What did she have that was so special?*

China was finally composed, and had completely switched personalities before speaking her next few words. The detective could tell she was having some disturbing emotional issues and was thinking hard. Maybe searching for some pertinent information.

"Where was his ex-girlfriend, Carlie?" she finally asked, emphasizing the word *ex*.

"We don't know," Peters answered. He became more excited than a child with a new toy. He loved the fact that China mentioned Carlie's name. "You think she had something to do with the shooting? Did Kirk mention her? Has she been to see you? Call you? Anything?" He never gave China a chance to cut in.

China liked where all of this was going. She loved the attention. Peters signaled for the other detectives to come inside the room, and he dished out hushed instructions before sending them on their way.

"They did have a few arguments," China finally stated.

All other conversation in the room stopped. "What else do you know lil' lady?" Travis searched for more.

"I know that Kirk left her for me, and she didn't like it." China rolled her neck around and copped a serious attitude, like she really meant what she was saying. "Hell, she might be tryna get me too." She smiled inside at her shameless lie.

Suddenly Peters was called to the door. While he stood talking with his back to China, she knew he was getting some important news by the way his head nodded up and down. She put her hands together for the first time ever, and prayed that Kirk had lived. Through Peters' legs, the white coat told her it was a doctor. Maybe Kirk's doctor.

Before she knew it, the outdated detective grinned. "Well, it looks like he might make it. Paralyzed from the waist down, but he'll make it."

China's heart dropped to her stomach. *Paralyzed?* She grabbed her stomach, thinking about the life of her child. *What would Kirk's life be like?*

How would she be able to take care of a newborn and a man in a wheelchair? Her thoughts ran wild as the brim of her eyelids filled with tears. *Yes, he was alive, but at what cost? He may as well be dead,* she thought.

China's heart thumped as the short Vietnamese doctor entered. "What 'bout his familiee? the doctor asked. "You know someone we can call?"

"Me." She paused before speaking hesitantly. "He has no one but me."

The doctor and Travis Peters looked at each other at the same time. "There's gotta be someone," Peters asked again.

"Just me and our little one." China leaned back in the bed to rest. She had a decision to make. Kirk needed her, but could she handle the pressure?

Chapter
• • • • • • • • • •
22

It was shortly after 9 p.m. when Rico swiped the key through the magnetic strip. He hated spending money at the Sheraton when the Howard Johnson was perfect for what he was there to do. The Ho-Jo was what he'd called it in the past, but for Carlie, that spot wouldn't do.

As soon as the hotel door opened, he went to work. He pulled three victory cigars from his duffle bag and lined them up on the circular table in the corner of the room. His plan was to smoke one just after banging Carlie's back out, and the other two he and Devon would smoke together.

Although Rico wanted Carlie, he hated women who tried to be sneaky. Trick, gold-digger and hoe, was the perfect stage name for Carlie at that moment. Loyal women were a must where he came from. Carlie giving up the punanie wasn't cool, and Devon needed to know about it. Of course, after he handled business.

Rico moved quickly after getting the call from Carlie, saying she was on her way up. He had talked to her hours before and got excited about the freaky conversation they had. The more he reminisced, the hornier he became. He rushed to the mirror, checking his appearance from both sides. The scent from his cologne satisfied him enough not to spray for the fifth time. Everything was right, until he patted his pocket, "Oh fuck! I forgot my fuckin' condoms," he mumbled.

He scrambled through the bag, realizing they weren't there. Instantly, he jetted to meet Carlie at the door, because as soon as she made it to the room, he was going to the store.

Just as he opened the door, they both stared each other eye to eye for about twenty seconds before speaking. Suddenly, Rico's sexy persona disappeared. The lumps and bruises protruding from Carlie's face had him in shock. It hadn't been that long ago since he'd talked to her, and she surely didn't mention it on the phone. He looked down the hall, rotating from right to left several times before feeling sure no one was after her.

Instantly, he forgot about the condoms as Carlie took a step forward. She brushed pass him, inviting herself in.

"Well, hello to you too," she finally said.

The ice-breaker was still a bit tense, but enough to snap Rico from his thoughts.

"Devon, Kirk, or someone else?" he asked, looking at the tight jeans that showed off most of her skin just below her belly. If she were his woman, someone would be fucked up right now. He grabbed Carlie by her shoulders lightly. He wasn't sure if she was tender or ready for what he had planned.

"What happened?" he questioned.

Carlie bounced toward the bed, like she was in the mood

to party. Within moments, she pulled an incredible magic act and stripped down to a pink and black strapless lingerie set. Even though she hurt deep inside, she moved full steam ahead with her plan.

"Come over here, sexy," she called.

Rico felt funny about pre-planning how to fuck and destroy a visibly bruised woman. It seemed as though she'd already been through enough. He kissed her on the neck, trying to ignore the bruises.

"Ummm, you smell so good. I'm glad you finally called."

Carlie kissed back nervously. She wondered whether the time was right to break the news. Hoping that her clever idea might keep her from going all the way, she moved in odd positions, showing off her bruises. She needed Rico to ask more questions. She needed to expose Devon with it seeming like the information had to be pried out of her. Or would it matter? Rico might want to fuck, regardless of hearing about Devon.

With her last chance in front of her, she raised her hand to caress his face. Just as she began to rub, Rico noticed the beat up, dark disgusting lines on her nails. He knew an injury like that could've only come from blood being trapped between the nail plate and the nail bed.

"You gotta be truthful, tell me what happened?" he asked. "I know somethin' is up." He nodded. "I wanna help you." "You're helping me now." She smiled a half-ass smile. Rico's arm didn't need to be twisted too much. He unbuckled his pants and pushed Carlie forcefully toward the ground. She gagged, realizing she was between his knees. At first, she thought she was brave enough to carry out her plan. Surely, if she had to fuck Rico, she would, but her lips wasn't touching shit. She twitched, trying to come up with something quick.

The moment she glanced over at his duffle bag, she had crazy thoughts. What if he had duct tape in the bag? What if he was some sex maniac and wanted to tie her to the bed? Hell, what if she decided not to live up to all the nasty gestures she'd dished out over the last few days? Would he want to kill her? Or beat her like Devon had?

"We gotta talk," she said, grabbing his hand. She started to raise up from off her knees.

Rico's right hand put firm pressure on her shoulder, sending her body back toward the floor. "About what? You wanna tell daddy what happened to your beautiful face?" As usual he wanted to be in control.

"Yep. As a matter of fact, I do." Carlie thought Rico cupping her chin was a sign of affection, so she played it up. If academy awards were being given out, she would've won by a long shot. She flipped personalities faster than a blackjack dealer flipping cards on a table.

"It's because of you," she said. "I was trying to save you."

"Get the fuck outta here," he said jokingly. "Why would you need to save me?" He gave Carlie a disapproving look, like he wanted a good explanation. He moved back just a little, giving her some breathing room.

"It's Devon," she cried, like an actress in a star role. "He knew I was gonna tell you, so he beat me!" She took the quick opportunity to stand.

"Tell me what?" he asked slowly. Rico grabbed Carlie tightly by the back of her neck. What she was hinting at didn't sound too kosher, so he wanted to be one hundred percent clear. He gritted through his teeth like she was now the enemy. "Tell me now!"

"He's a snitch!"

"Hell, the fuck no! He can't be!" His hands flew up in the air. Then sudden swift gestures followed. Rico stood, then sat. He stood again and paced the floor. "Tell me how you know. Wait, you fuckin' knew this the other day?"

"No," she answered quickly. "I found out yesterday. He told me in between my ass whipping." She looked for sympathy from Rico, but it wasn't working.

He tossed ideas around his head, like a juggler at the circus. He really didn't care what had happened to Carlie, the concern was why.

"I gotta get the fuck outta here. You checked to make sure nobody followed you?"

"Of course I did. You think I wanna get whipped again." Carlie needed to make Rico trust her. She reached for his hand, but he had no intentions of latching on. "He was supposed to make you buy from him. You know, set you up. But it doesn't seem like the feds are too happy about the case. Maybe they don't have anything on you." She hunched her shoulders.

"Put your shit on," he said, pointing to Carlie's clothes scattered on the bed. "We leavin'," he said, sitting down to collect his thoughts.

Carlie wasn't sure what she had accomplished. It seemed like Rico was more scared than in retaliation mode. She needed Devon done for good this time. Running from him wasn't good enough, and jail wasn't good enough, death was the only solution. She loved the hell out of Devon, but she had to start loving herself more.

Rico was like a mute pup, as fear spread across his face.

He reached for his phone and punched over thirty number combinations into the calculator. Thirty-two thousand, twelve-thousand, three-thousand, fifty-thousand. He punched for over a minute before stopping. The total, one hundred eighty thousand on the street, and over one hundred fifty thousand in his safe. Clearly, it wasn't enough for a Columbian on the run.

Rico thought about the money he had been sending to his family in Columbia. Two to three thousand was wired monthly to take care of his mother and thirteen-year-old brother. In addition some of that money was supposed to be put away just in case Rico needed to hide out near his home town.

Supposedly, Rico's mother had everything set up just in case he had to come home. But by the way she begged for money on a regular basis, he figured there wasn't much money stashed. With so much frustration building up, Rico wanted to shout. He needed more money and more time, but assumed he couldn't get either. The fact remained he didn't know how much Devon had told them, or what Devon really knew.

"Damn, damn, damn!" he yelled, while hitting his forehead. "I should've known that mufucka didn't get out on no fuckin' technicality." Rico had never introduced Devon to his connection, so they were clearly after him. He glanced over at Carlie, who was now moving like molasses dripping from a bottle. "Hurry the fuck up!" he yelled. "It didn't take that long to take that shit off!"

"I'm not the one to be mad at," she snapped back. Carlie continued to put her clothes on slowly, trying to buy herself some time. "You know he saw us together," she stated.

She looked over and saw Rico kneeling over in the chair like he was praying. She'd seen that same scenario many times before with her clients. It was unbelievable. No matter how rough they claim to be, tough guys broke down instantly at the thought of doing a long bid. There was no sympathy for Rico either. *They were all the same,* she thought.

As she looked closer, she could see Rico was in deep thought. Carlie never expected him to contemplate this much. She had assumed the only decision to make would be to decide which gun to use.

"Did you hear me, Rico?" she asked, moving closer.

He shook his head, but never looked up. Her voice deepened. She had to persuade Rico there were no other options for Devon.

"He saw me talking to you because he was watching us, along with the feds. Actually you." She pointed at Rico, to make sure he got the point. "They were watching you. Devon saw me and went crazy. He left the officers and chased me to our hotel. If it weren't for the officers, my ass would be dead." It was pissing Carlie off the way Rico just nodded. "Are you getting any of this?"

"No doubt," he said, with a bit of sarcasm. "So, why didn't he kill you?"

Her hands straddled her bare hips. Rico's eyes followed, but the interest was gone. At the moment, he was more worried about being handcuffed and sent upstate than getting wet.

"So, he beat you first, and then volunteered information about snitching?" Rico was starting to sound like he didn't believe her.

"No" she snapped. "He actually told me he was watching

you because I lied. I had told him I was at the spa, but since he saw me, I guess he wanted to prove it."

"Are you lyin' now?"

"I'm trying to help you!"

"Sure. Did you lie about Kirk?"

That was it. Carlie was done. She grabbed her purse and headed for the door, but Rico was two steps behind her. He didn't trust her as far as he could see her. For all he knew, as soon as she left the room, the feds would be coming in after him. Carlie opened the door, and he slammed it back.

"Did you lie about Kirk?" he shouted, with killer eyes.

"No," she answered, with a straight face. "I could care less what happens to Kirk, but I didn't have to tell lies on him. He's truly a fucked up person."

"Bet. I hope you not fuckin' with me, lil' lady. I was gonna have Kirk handled, but somebody called his phone and the police answered." Rico looked even more confused than before. "I thought maybe somebody else just wanted that mufucka dead, too. But hell, I don't know now. Maybe the police got his ass in custody too."

Carlie hunched her shoulders and flipped back into role-playing 101. She looked just as confused as Rico.

"Hell if I know," she answered, as Rico moved away from the door. "Whatever happens, I'm sure it's what he deserves." She smiled inside, knowing that her money was well spent. She just hoped her exact instructions were followed. "Be safe," she stated, like she really cared.

Chapter
• • • • • • • • • •
23

Carlie sat in the courtroom listening to Williard make a fool of himself. She watched him raise his voice, trying to point out unproven incidents that never really happened the night Saundra Kelly was killed. Marcus had finally come clean and Williard had a feeling he was about to lose the case. The rumors floating around the courthouse said, Williard was worried sick that Marcus was going to leave a free man. He knew there was something big going on that he didn't know about.

The moment Williard looked over his shoulder, eye-balling Carlie, Ricky and Marcus, Carlie turned her head. As he rambled on about nothing, her mind drifted away to everything that had happened over the last week. Fortunately, it was becoming a blur for her.

While her bruises hadn't healed completely, her mind and soul had. The painful memories of Devon beating her one last time somehow made her stronger. She still had a few uneasy feelings about him showing his face again, but had confidence in either Don sending him back to jail, or Rico killing him dead. Either one would work. One thing was certain, if he showed up once more, Carlie was calling in Ricky's ruthless connection *again*.

Instantly, her thoughts switched to her teenage years. She remembered nights when suspicious-looking men would have business meetings with her father until the wee hours of the morning. Back then, she had no idea they were hit-men. The only background she'd been told about Ricky was that he struggled to become a successful lawyer. It wasn't until her early twenties that she learned he'd once been a hired killer. Although wrong, his firm instructions and large payments got the jobs done. It had worked for him, and now it had worked for her too.

Carlie smiled and folded her hands in front of her as Williard approached the bench. She pretended to pay attention, but was thinking about the hit she put on Kirk. She loved the fact that she was able to handpick how she wanted him shot up. She remembered specifically writing her instructions and requesting that he lived. Carlie wanted him paralyzed. She figured the suffering would be crueler than being shot dead. Besides, being dead wouldn't have given him the chance to have to pay her money back. Carlie had already hired the best lawyer possible, and forgery charges were already filed.

In all, she was pleased. The only thing that could have made the situation better was for her to see Kirk bleed and squirm with her own eyes. Carlie laughed inside at how everyone pegged her to be so stupid. Yes, she was dumb and shouldn't have put up with Kirk, but she was trying to have a semi-normal life. A life where her father would be pleased with the way she turned out. A life filled with children and certainly no beatings from her husband.

The quick reaction to heads turning toward the back of the courtroom caught Carlie's attention. She sat up straight looking toward the aisle. Chief Jordan entered, and sat in a space near the front that had been reserved especially for him. He and Ricky met several times over the last week to review the new evidence. Since the Chief made it perfectly clear during the early part of the trial that he expected Marcus to be convicted, Ricky decided to show him evidence in advance why Marcus wasn't guilty. The Chief understood, and agreed to appear at the trial for support. After all, the city wanted justice and so did the families involved.

Behind the Chief, Mr. and Mrs. Dupree sat, anxiously waiting for Carlie to take the floor. They had listened to Williard go on and on, and wanted the world to know the truth about their son. Marcus sat stiffly with a worried expression. He wasn't sure if he was headed for the gas chamber, or soon to be released. He eased up just a bit as his lawyers prepared to stand.

When Carlie took the floor she was more confident than ever before. She paced back and forth before calling Marcus Dupree to the stand. The moment Marcus raised his right hand and agreed to the oath, Carlie turned to look at Williard, who sat impatiently with his arms crossed. He looked irritated and wondered what she had up her sleeve.

As the questioning session began, Carlie sounded so sure of herself. At first, she asked basic questions with yes or no answers to clarify the relationship between Saundra and Marcus. Then, slowly she proceeded with more complex questions, which had the jury wondering where this was all going.

"Did you shoot and kill your girlfriend?" she blurted out.

Marcus didn't even flinch. "No I did not," he responded.

"Did you ever beat or abuse your girlfriend?"

Marcus hesitated before speaking. "Yes, I hit her once or twice," he said, in a sincere tone.

The atmosphere in the courtroom became noisier than usual. From the muffled comments heard, Carlie could tell most people thought even worse about Marcus than they did before coming to court. But Carlie kept grilling him like she knew what she was doing.

"Did she ever beat you?" Carlie asked.

"I wouldn't call it that," he answered.

"Yes or no," she stated firmly. "Did she ever beat you?"

"Objection Your Honor," Williard stood to say. "This is ridiculous. What does it have to do with the case?"

"Sir, if I may," she said, grabbing a folder from Ricky's hand and waiting for approval to approach the bench. "I have here many police reports which proves that Saundra Kelly beat and abused Marcus Dupree on several instances. It has a lot to do with the case," she barked in Williard's direction. "I also have several witness' from Ms. Kelly's family who are here and ready to take the stand." Carlie's voice had become so strong and aggressive, that everyone in the courtroom sensed her commitment to getting to the bottom of things. "So again, it has a lot to do with the case!" she ended.

"Your Honor...," Williard said, shaking his head.

"Excuse me, sir. I believe I was speaking." Carlie stood up against Williard like Holyfield against Tyson. This was her chance to show her father she was far from stupid, tired of letting men overpower her, and capable of winning the case.

"Continue Ms. Stewart," the judge said, taking off his glasses. His puckered brow and curious expression showed he was very interested in hearing what Carlie had to say.

"Did she ever beat you?" she asked Marcus again.

Carlie gave Marcus an evil look. They had prepared questions and practiced for several hours earlier in the morning. Marcus expressed how embarrassed he was to admit that Saundra, *a woman*, had been beating him with her huge fist. The reports said she whipped him with belts and extension cords, and had even stabbed him once.

Domestic violence is normally thought to consist of men beating on women, but Saundra was strong, and had repeatedly threatened and physically abused Marcus regularly. He had told Carlie about his embarrassment and never wanted to really tell what actually happened that night. Carlie assured him the truth would change the outcome of the entire trial, but if he didn't tell, he'd be in jail for a long time. She and Ricky were hoping for a mistrial, and an acquittal would be a miracle.

Marcus finally spoke softly. "Yes, she fought me," he said hesitantly.

"But did she hurt you, or put bruises on you?"

Marcus hated to admit it. He didn't want to seem like a punk, but it was time to be honest. "Yes," he admitted.

"Yes, Marcus. We know she did," Carlie responded, with sympathy. "We have several police reports and pictures to show the bruises and stab wounds." Carlie winked at Ricky. "I'm done, Your Honor. Williard can cross-exam," she snickered. "And then, I'd like to call our surprise witness, Mr. Charles Kelly."

Williard stopped in his tracks. He was completely choked

up by her last comment. *What would Saundra Kelly's father have to say?* he thought. *He should be a grieving father right now.* "No need to cross-exam," he said to the judge.

The hushed tones in the courtroom turned into loud chatter. Charles Kelly, who was Saundra Kelly's father and Chief Jordan's brother, stood up. He walked toward the stand with his head downward, unable to look Marcus in the eye. Before Carlie knew it, he was sworn in and wore a grim look, like he was ready to break down on the stand.

Carlie moved quickly toward Mr. Kelly. Something didn't seem right. Before she could get her first question out, he burst out into tears. "My baby, my baby, my baby!" he called out. "Lord knows I loved her," he said. "But she put a hurting on that boy!" Carlie turned to see Mr. Kelly's finger pointing at Marcus. "I knew for a long time she was torturing him. I was there plenty of nights when she called the police on'em after whipping his ass. She would haul off and hit him like she wanted to kill'em!"

Carlie's eyes looked like they wanted to pop out her head. She didn't know what to say next. She had expected to ask about the night he was a witness when Saundra stabbed Marcus. Mr. Kelly even went with Marcus to the hospital and suggested that he take pictures. "Uh…"

Ricky gave Carlie a signal, saying that Mr. Kelly was doing fine on his own. So, Carlie prolonged her next question, allowing him to finish.

"I was on the phone!" he yelled.

"The night of the murder?"

"Yes sir'ree." He shook his head and made strange moaning sounds in between his words. "She took that gun, ready to shoot Marcus with it. He banged and banged on her front

door, while I was on the phone. She told me she was gon'
either beat his ass good or shoot'em dead." Mr. Kelly cried
and cried until he was escorted from the stand.

Some jurors were outraged and cried discreetly along
with Mr. Kelly. Although Marcus felt like a fool, he cried too.
But Carlie stood strong. She was ready to get to the bottom
of things. Within moments, she'd put all the pieces of the
puzzle together, and re-created the night Saundra Kelly was
murdered.

It came out that Marcus was actually reacting in self-
defense on the night of the shooting. Marcus finally told
everyone that he went there in a jealous rage, thinking that
Saundra had another man at the house. But Saundra met
him at the door and fired the first shot at him. She missed,
and he in return, grabbed the gun and shot her in self-
defense. Saundra was a 280-pound woman, and couldn't easily be calmed down, especially with a gun, he told everyone
sadly.

Marcus' pride was crushed. *A grown ass man running from
a woman*, he thought. He wondered if he should've done
things differently. As Carlie and Williard talked privately
with the judge, Marcus could feel the stares of several people.
It seemed that every man in the room looked at him strangely, like they wanted to ask him what kind of punk are you.

Marcus twitched for a moment, like he regretted telling
the truth. While his hands shook with anticipation, he kept
his eyes on Carlie's every move. He deeply trusted her, and
could tell she was at the bench fighting for his best interest.
Earlier, she'd told him briefly about her experience with an
abusive mate, and told him he'd heal, both mentally and
physically. "It would definitely take time, but it will happen,"

she boasted.

Before long, Carlie turned to face Marcus and Ricky. She grinned widely and headed toward them, performing like a football player after running a major play. She mouthed the word *mistrial,* just as the judge banged his gravel.

The spectators went wild in the courtroom after hearing the verdict. In all, the jurors, the judge, and anyone in attendance, knew there were too many witnesses and evidence that showed Saundra Kelly could've been trying to kill Marcus Dupree. For now, it was a mistrial and Carlie had defeated Williard.

Carlie blushed when Ricky cupped her chin. "You did well, baby girl."

"Good job to you too," she responded. "I want to thank you, Dad. I couldn't have done this without you." She looked over and smiled at her accomplishment. Marcus was in the middle of a circle, surrounded by family and friends.

"Yes, you could. I have faith in you. At least you learned an important lesson during this case that you can share with your children one day."

"What's that?" Carlie frowned.

"Stay away from bad boys. They grow up to be dangerous men."

They both laughed and walked out the courtroom.

Chapter
• • • • • • • • • • •
24

Just before daylight, Rico scrambled to throw his last minute items into one of the three luggage bags. Unable to see clearly, he stepped on unwanted clothes and old accessories, trying to hurry. The sunlight was due to come up soon, and he wanted to be gone just before daybreak. Hangers had been thrown all across the floor, and his closet looked like it had been raided. He ran to the living room to grab one more thing, when he stopped to acknowledge how empty, yet untidy, the house looked.

Over the last week, word had spread quickly through Rico's camp that he was leaving the country. Friends, associates, and the few family members living in the U.S., gathered like roaches at his house, to collect anything he was giving away. They all left happily with furniture, dishes, flat screen televisions, and plenty of guns. You name it, they had it, and left his house a mess in the process.

Rico wasn't concerned with material things. He'd always had just about anything money could buy. For now, he focused on the technical issues; his passport, plane ticket and money, which was all intact. Big Tex was taking him to the airport, and a third of his

money needed to be strapped on him, both tightly and unnoticeable to make it through security. The other money had already been buried in a safe place until he returned from Columbia.

At the thought of money, Rico grabbed his nylon back brace and strapped it around his lower back area. Frantically, he searched for the Nike duffle bag. For seconds, he threw things around in a panic, unable to find the bag. Suddenly, he spotted it, threw it up on the bed, and unzipped it. Inside, he grabbed pre-bundled stacks of hundreds, fifties and twenties, and placed them strategically inside his back brace.

For two days, he'd practiced how to place one hundred and twenty thousand dollars securely inside against his skin, yet without altering the shape of his body. He knew airport security had been heightened since 9/11, especially at Newark Airport. So he took every precaution to make sure when he went through the metal detector, the money inside the brace wouldn't be detected. One advantage was that he'd chartered a plane, so he wouldn't be going through the same checkpoint as those who traveled on major airlines.

Feeling like an overstuffed kangaroo, he jetted over to the window and pulled the curtain back to see if Big Tex was out front yet. Like clockwork, 5:30 a.m., and he was pulling up. Rico's mind raced. He tried to make sure he remembered everything that was necessary. Most loose ends had been tied up shortly after Carlie informed him that Devon was working with the police. But he wanted to be one hundred percent sure there was nothing else.

With no more delays, Rico zipped all three bags and rolled the larger suitcase to the front door. The drapes were light enough to see Big Tex waiting through the window. Rico wondered why his big ass didn't come inside to help with the bags. He ran to the back room, and returned within moments, carrying the last two pieces of luggage.

Just as he opened the door and struggled to set the largest suitcase outside on the porch, he noticed the sun starting to peek through. To his surprise, the small spec of light complimented the red and blue strobe lights headed his way.

Rico stood motionless on the porch. He was spell-bound. No sirens sounded, but the motorcade of vans, undercover vehicles, and squad cars pulled up like the militia coming to get Bin Laden. He couldn't catch an accurate count as they hit the corner, going fifty miles per hour, but six to seven cars was his guess. Rico glanced at the truck, expecting Tex to pull off like a fucking cowboy, but he sat still.

With the jump-out boys only four yards away, his thoughts spun in circles. Rico thought about running back inside to grab a gun. *Shooting his way out was a possibility*. He wasn't exactly sure how many cops were in the cars that had just rolled up out front. He took two steps back, dismissing the thought of going for a gun. It suddenly clicked, *he'd given them all away*. Just then another crazy thought popped in his head, *a butcher knife*. "Stupid—ass thought," he said out loud.

Rico had no idea that Don and his boys had kept a close eye on him over the last few days, and had a legal wire-tap on his cell phone. Although Rico never mentioned drugs, he did say that his flight was leaving town at 8:30 a.m. out of Newark to Bogotá, Columbia. So, with the search warrant in hand, and the intent on finding drugs and bringing Rico in, every member of the unit jumped out with their guns drawn, ready for action.

A feeling of defeat ran through Rico's body as he watched two officers escort Big Tex from the truck in handcuffs. It was at that moment, he realized he was caught and outnumbered.

While still on the porch in the twilight zone, he ignored the red-hair officer on the ground yelling, "Put your hands above your head!"

Officer Chaney, Don's right-hand man, moved closer toward Rico. "We got him," he said, happily into the walkie-talkie.

Don didn't respond, he just laughed out loud so deeply, the officers nearby could hear. Don couldn't be there, but gave specific instructions to make sure Rico was apprehended correctly. He also wanted step-by-step details given to him over the walkie-talkie. He didn't want any mishaps, no slip-ups with reading Rico his rights, no shoot-outs, and definitely no chases. He did expect Chaney to call Channel 9 news once the drugs and money found at Rico's house was seized. Don knew he would get promoted, and in return, he promised to promote Chaney too.

They expected to find several kilos of cocaine and hundreds of thousands of dollars. Therefore, they were all pumped.

Chaney had followed Rico for so many months, he felt like he knew him personally.

"Come on down!" he shouted. "It's over."

Rico looked at Chaney and the officers strangely, who had now formed a semi-circle around the house. The look in his eyes showed he wasn't too sure he wanted to surrender.

"Get your hands up, boy," Chaney said.

Rico's hands didn't go up. He stood glassy-eyed.

"There are no options!" the youngest member of the surveillance team shouted. He spoke in a matter-of-fact tone, like he was ready to bust off a bullet. As a matter of fact, all of the younger jump-out boys were ready for whatever moves Rico made. They were used to chases, and loved beating the drug-boys to a pulp.

"Lay down on the ground!" the red-hair officer shouted, moving closer like an actor on the Matrix. His gun was cocked, and his expression showed he wasn't playing.

Chaney stood by his side with his gun drawn too, but not as emotional. "Blast his ass if he makes the wrong move," he said to the young, anxious officer. "Get on the ground, now!" he called out to Rico.

Chaney put one foot on the bottom of the four-step staircase, waiting for Rico to make a move. He couldn't see any visible signs of a gun, and was ready to make his way up the other three stairs. Rico finally looked him dead in the eye.

"Down, now," Chaney said, in a calm, slow tone. Even though they both looked like they understood one another, the moment Rico bent toward the ground, another fiery plainclothes officer budded in.

"Hands behind your head, motherfucker!" he shouted.

Before Chaney could reach the next step, the officer with red-hair leaped onto the porch from the side and knocked Rico to the ground. He pressed forcefully into his neck with the tip of his shoe, forcing Rico's lips to kiss the ground. The extra force wasn't necessary. In his mind, Rico had already given up peacefully, but the function of his brain just wouldn't allow his hands to rise in the air.

All of a sudden, the plainclothes officer brushed past Chaney and whipped out his cuffs. Chaney was shocked at the way the younger officers were so eager to handle the situation. They went wild trying to be the heroes, when all along, Don would eventually get the credit.

"It's over," he said, into the walkie-talkie. But he got no response from Don. He diverted his attention to the task ahead of him. "Get in there!" Chaney yelled out to his team of officers, pointing to the door. "Lay everything out on the table." He grinned, "And I do mean everything; the drugs, money, scales, paraphernalia, everything." He looked over at one of the other officers. "You did make that call to the reporter, didn't you?"

"Sure did, sir," the officer answered.

Just as a slew of officers jetted inside the house, Chaney pulled Rico from the ground and smiled. "You have the right to remain silent. Anything you say may be used against you in a court of law. You have the right to consult an attorney before speaking. If you cannot afford an attorney..."

Hearing those chilling words made Rico shake his head.

"Don't shake your head, son. We're gonna be on T.V." Chaney smirked as he saw the news truck turning the corner. "Hell, this is gon' be the biggest drug-bust of all times, and these cock suckas are late," he said. He led Rico to the car with his hands cuffed behind his back.

Within moments, one of Chaney's most trusted officers appeared in the doorway. The disappointing look on his face told Chaney he wouldn't be pleased. The cameras had already started rolling, so he didn't want to yell. Instead, he shook his head and gave the cut sign below his chin.

Chaney handed Rico off to one of the other officers and

flew toward the house. "No guns, no drugs, no money, nothing," the officer whispered. "The house is nearly cleaned out. He must've stashed everything somewhere else."

Chaney grinned widely at the reporter. "Cut the camera. We gotta talk," he said. Instantly, he got on the walkie-talkie and told Don the bad news.

Even though Rico made them look bad in front of the cameras, the evidence was already built against him. He was definitely going to jail for a long, long time. Rico thought about telling Chaney about the money that was wrapped around his body, but decided against it. He didn't want them to have a thing to make them look good in front of the cameras. He preferred the money be found at the station. Just in case his lawyer wanted to try and get it back.

* * *

Thirty miles away, Devon slept lightly in his efficiency, waiting for the call from Don. He was somewhat happy about getting another chance to set Rico up. He regretted running off of the case, and especially felt guilty about putting his hands on Carlie. Don had told him that he'd cut him some slack if he still helped them nail Rico. But they wanted blood, concrete evidence. They wanted Devon to make Rico verbally admit to selling him drugs.

The case was being built with the best investigators, as many informants as possible, and most of all, Snake. Snake would be a key witness for the prosecution, and had already been picked up and enrolled in the witness protection program.

As Devon slept, he had no idea that the deal was over and

an unmarked car was out front, waiting to transport him back to prison. After Don got word that Rico was skipping town, he made plans to roll on both Rico and Devon in the early hours, a perfect time for jump-outs. Devon's days on the street were over and he didn't even know it.

The sound of someone ramming the front door and knocking it from its hinges sent Devon leaping from his mattress. He jumped for his gun that sat underneath his shirt on a nearby table, but never got two steps away from his bed. He was knocked back down onto the mattress by someone he'd never seen before.

Instead of twelve officers deep, the way they rolled on Rico, Devon got rolled on by Don and three big, burly officers. The two unfamiliar officers stood before him, with guns drawn, but Don banged a small baton looking object back and forth across his palm.

Devon hit himself repeatedly, trying to wake up. He wanted to be sure his door had really been knocked down. This was no nightmare, it was real. Don stood in front of him like a stick-up kid and not 5.0.

"Mannnnn, what's up with you knockin' the damn door down!" he roared.

"Nigga, don't use that tone. I told you before you ain't the man. I am."

"You think you gon' hit me with that?" Devon asked, in a bull-like tone.

"Your skummy-ass ain't worth it. I don't know whose decision it was to let you the fuck out anyway." Don's face scrunched up like Devon had killed his mama, or committed some unforgivable act.

Something was different about Don. Devon could tell he

wasn't there with good news, and he wasn't there to make friends. And he damn sure wasn't acting like he was ready to go. He seemed more upset than he'd ever seen him before.

"Man, let me get my shit on. If you was ready to roll on Rico, all you had to do was say so. Breakin' down doors wasn't necessary."

"We're not going to see Rico," Don stated.

"Then, what the hell am I up at 6 a.m. for?"

When Don waved the handcuffs in Devon's direction, he started to get the picture. "You sendin' me back?" he yelled.

"That's right, playa," he said angrily.

"Why I gotta go back? I did my part." He looked around the room for approval. The other two officers stood like mannequins in a store window. "You...you...said yourself, you got enough evidence to convict."

Don looked at Devon with disgust and shook his head.

"Man, what?" Devon asked. "You got a personal vendetta with me? 'Cause me runnin' off the case didn't do no harm."

"It's not about the case no more. You already fucked that up. You see, we had a chance to get more evidence. Rico may have even sold you some shit directly. But now we'll never know, will we?"

"C'mon, mannnnnnnnn..."

"Shut the fuck up. Your ass turned out to be like a nuclear bomb. When you working the right way, motherfuckin' drug dealers better watch out, but when you running around like a loose cannon, you can cause a catastrophe."

"What the fuck is that supposed to mean?" Devon looked confused.

"It means you never really did shit. All we learned from

you, we already knew. Even your man Snake helped us out more than you."

"Snake?" Devon looked shocked.

"Yeah, Snake. You'll see him in court. Y'all will look like twins in court, testifying in orange jumpsuits." Even though Don meant for his comment to be a joke, he didn't crack a smile. This case meant a lot to him personally, and to his image on the force.

"I'm gonna look like a fool down at headquarters," he blurted out, in a rage. "I bragged for days about how my press conference would go when I caught Rico with all his drugs, guns and money. But you fucked all that up!"

"How you gon' blame that shit on me? I can't make Rico keep drugs on him. I can't make him have a gun!"

"Too bad, cause you're going back."

"The hell I am."

"What you say, playa?"

"You heard me. I was locked up for five years, I know what it's like." Devon's voice started to sadden.

"Get sad on me if you want, cause there ain't no sympathy here. You know how it goes. Besides, where you're going is safer than being on the streets. Right about now Officer Chaney is probably telling Rico that you're a snitch. He's in handcuffs as we speak, and you'll probably meet up with him in central booking. "

Devon's heart thumped. The impact of the news made him stumble just a bit. Now he'd never be able to walk the streets again with his head held high. Everyday he'd have to look over his shoulder. So many thoughts crowded in Devon's head. Going back to jail meant he'd never get a chance to make things right with Carlie, nor get back at Kirk.

It was apparent his heart was in pain. He looked like a griev-ing husband who'd lost his wife forever.

"Put your clothes on, and let's go," Don ordered.

Devon paused before running his hands over his face harshly. He was so confused. *Would Rico have him killed?* His sane mind told him escaping wasn't an option, and he should put his clothes on and go peacefully. But the crazy side of Devon told him to say, *fuck going back to jail.*

He backed up toward where his shirt lay, keeping his good eye on Don, who was acting so psychotic. Devon even thought he might try to shoot him in the back if he turned around. Devon had flashbacks of prison, as he reached for his shirt. He was almost in a daze, just as Don hit the baton into his hand one last time, reminding him of the ruthless C.O.'s.

The next thing Don knew, Devon had grabbed his gun from beneath his shirt, turned it in his direction, and blew his brains to the west side of New York!

Chapter
• • • • • • • • • • •
25

Six months later, the day came that everyone had been waiting for. China gave birth to a beautiful, six-pound baby girl at exactly 2:08 p.m., named Kyla. All day she hovered over her newborn and reacted to her every move. Every time she was taken to the nursery, China went ballistic. She wanted her to stay close by her side every minute of the hour. No one could've ever explained to China about the special connection a mother has to a child. Deep in her gut, she now knew what it was like to see her true love.

For hours she sang made up lullabies, and caressed the upper part of her baby girl's back. Anyone who knew China personally would've asked, *who in hell is this woman?* She had done a complete three sixty, and acted like she'd been a loving and caring person all her life. Luckily for Kirk, the nurse walked in to do some vitals on China, which forced her to hand the baby over to him.

"Oh, don't breathe too closely on her," she instructed.

The nurse on duty had already learned to ignore China's

obsessive remarks. "It's his baby, too," she remarked.

"It is. But he doesn't know what to do," she stated softly. "Did he wash his hands?" China asked. She didn't want to hurt Kirk's feelings, but would do it if it meant protecting her baby. She was starting to irritate everyone. "Make sure you hold her head up," she called out, as the nurse eased her bed downward.

China nearly fell out of bed trying to peek and see what Kirk was doing. Kyla had obviously consumed her mind and time. Although Kirk was there, sitting by her side, he wasn't even thought about. All day, he sat in his wheelchair like an outsider on a friendly visit. No one would've known he was the father if she hadn't resembled him so much.

As Kirk held his baby girl in his arms, he thought about how her birth changed everything for him. His entire outlook on life was different. Being paralyzed had already changed a lot and left him a limited amount of options. The street life was over. Surely, he couldn't sell drugs from his car on wheels. Nor did he have the time.

Every minute of the day was spent working at a telemarketing agency selling medical equipment to benefit the handicapped. And every week, half of his check was deducted and sent to Carlie. That was a slap on the hand compared to what Carlie's lawyer went for. All the cars on his lot, and any other assets, had to be sold. Every red cent missing from Carlie's money had to be paid back. In light of all his troubles, when he looked into Kyla's eyes, nothing else mattered. He was hooked. If he had milk ducts, he would've breastfed.

China's bed rose just after the nurse finished updating her chart. She watched Kirk interact with their daughter. She had never seen him so sensitive before. Maybe that's why she felt a bit of sadness for him when she stated aggressively, "I'll take her now."

Kirk thought about not handing her over. He'd heard the nurse tell China the pill she'd given her would make her drowsy, and she probably wouldn't be able to keep her eyes open much longer. He knew that would be a good opportunity to hold his baby through the night. Instead, he handed her over and wheeled himself to the door.

"I'll see you tomorrow," he said.

China ignored him and kissed Kyla on the cheek. She began wrapping, then unwrapping her baby's blankets over and over again. She continued her obsessive behavior until she could take no more. When the nurse came by for her 3 a.m. check, she was defensive and over-protective.

"She just ate and is sound asleep." China smiled a wide smile. "Can you push her cot over here, please?"

"Why don't I take her over to the nursery?"

"The hell you will!" This was the first time she had reverted back to the old China. "She's stayin' right here with me!" she shouted.

"Ooookayyyy," the nurse mocked. "Now if you're sound asleep and can't hear her, then what?"

"I will hear her!" she shot back, in a demon-like tone.

"Your call," the nurse said, dimming the lights and heading out of the door. "Just remember you took two Tylenols with codeine and a heavy sleeping pill too. You just had a baby, child. You need some rest." The door shut and the room was completely silent.

China was glad the woman had left, but started to realize she was right. She closed her eyes, hoping to get some good rest before Kyla woke up in three hours screaming for milk.

China fell asleep before the medicine even kicked in. She slept like a baby, happy about her new position as a mother. She dreamt of walks to the park, fun days at the playground, and what Kyla's first day of pre-school would be like.

Hours passed, and a woman wearing a white lab coat entered the room and stood directly between China and Kyla. At first, it would've been assumed she was there for Kyla's 6 o'clock feeding. But suddenly, she moved closer to China, checking to see if she was sound asleep. She grinned inside, seeing China's chest moving up and down. *Sleep, honey, sleep*, she thought.

Instantly, the woman tip-toed over to the side of Kyla's plastic cot just a bit, and touched the baby gently. Careful not to make any noise, her movements were slow as she verified the tag around Kyla's ankle. She smiled and lifted the baby from the cot. In return, Kyla changed positions and twitched her innocent lips.

The woman suddenly moved away quickly, with the baby snugly in her arms, then paused. She moved backward, thinking to double-check the chart with rows of information. If she was going to snatch a baby from her cot, steal her, and be paid thousands for it, she couldn't afford a mix-up for that kind of money. The abductor smiled as she verified she indeed had the right baby.

Ten minutes later, the woman had finagled her way through the halls and down remote stairwells to avoid security and hospital employees. The 6 o'clock hour made the job easy, considering most workers were in a relaxed mode during the wee hours of the morning. As soon as the exit door opened to the outside parking lot, Carlie sat in her truck, waiting right outside the door.

The moment she saw what looked to be a nurse and a bundle in her arms, she knew there was a God. She jumped from her new Range Rover and hurried over to the woman. The two ladies made sure not to say a word to one another as they escorted Kyla to the back of the truck. Carlie opened the back door and signaled for Kyla to be put into the car seat. She had the seat inspected at the firehouse a few days ago, just like any good mother would. She felt at ease about having Kyla in the back alone.

Everything was perfect. Carlie grabbed the small pair of scissors from the front seat and clipped the identity tag from Kyla's ankle.

"There we go, all complete," she said to the woman.

The woman had her palm face-up, ready to be paid. "I think we should go now," she said hesitantly. "We did it, but hanging around would be stupid."

"You're right." She shut the back door and ran to the trunk of the car. Carlie popped the truck and rummaged through the tons of pink outfits, soft pastel colored blankets, pampers and cases of milk.

Carlie had the proud mama look when she turned to say, "You did the right thing. Just know that she'll be safe and loved." She smiled and handed off the thirty thousand dollars.

Carlie shut the trunk and ran to the driver's seat as the woman walked off. She wondered what would happen when China woke up to find her baby gone. She knew she'd covered all bases, and nothing would be tracked back to her. Carlie had been missing for over a month now. Once the Dupree case ended and Devon committed suicide, she worked herself to the bone, trying to put her crazy life behind her.

Four weeks ago, she convinced Ricky that she needed a break. *A real break.* Ricky agreed to find a replacement for Carlie so she could take the year long sabbatical she'd requested. She was supposedly already in Jamaica starting her extended vacation, and would be gone for a year. She wondered if someday China or Kirk would ever see her face-to-face again. Would she be able to look either one of them in the eye, and show off her new child?

Carlie drove away quickly without even putting on her seat belt. As she thought more and more about how she'd later pass Kyla off as her own, she lit up inside. She figured a year from now, she'd return home and tell Ricky the bad news. *She had a one-night stand and got pregnant,* she would say. Ricky would be pissed at her for not being married, but would be a wonderful, loving grandfather. At some point in life, she figured she would find the guts to tell him the truth.

Carlie stopped at a light and looked back at her new baby. She knew exactly what she was doing, and what the consequences would be if she got caught. The act was cruel and certainly illegal, but she was willing to take her chances. It was difficult to have sympathy for China since she had set out to steal her man and ruin her life. The more she thought about it, the more she realized China, Kirk and Devon had done her equally wrong. And they all had gotten what they deserved.

For the first time since Devon's funeral, Carlie was able to smile. Over the past few months, she had blamed herself for his death and slipped into a semi-state of depression. Sitting at the wheel, once again, she had flashbacks of Devon's picture sitting on the casket. The thought that his body was too messed up for an open casket, sent chills through her spine.

At one point in her life, she wanted Devon dead, as far under the ground as he could go. She didn't care if Rico did it, the police, or who pulled the trigger. It was the only way she could be assured he wouldn't ever beat her again.

Carlie knew the law. They say a battered woman has the option of leaving or calling the police, but not take matters into her own hands. Carlie had once considered using Ricky's connection to handle Devon. She knew she couldn't face him and be able to pull the trigger. It wasn't in her. Devon was like a magnet, and the attraction she had to him was dangerous.

In her heart, she knew he was better off dead, but the way it happened, bothered her. Knowing that he had killed himself often made her heart ache. It had been rumored at the funeral that he shot himself after finding out he couldn't be with Carlie ever again. She didn't really believe it, but occasionally her mind played tricks on her.

She expected to rejoice at his death, not be saddened by it. *I guess some things never change,* she thought. In all, her revenge felt good. For Kirk, the hit on his crippled ass, and stealing his baby, was more than enough payback. For China, she took her soul, and for Devon, he took his own. *The Ultimate Revenge.*

Carlie looked back at Kyla one last time as she put her blinker on, headed toward the highway. Suddenly, red and blue flashing lights raced behind her. Carlie panicked. She pressed the gas pedal with force, picking up speed like a race-car driver. Just as she pulled onto the ramp, she looked back at the police car, not noticing the *Do Not Enter* sign. The police were still rushing her way, but Carlie had no idea they weren't coming for her.

Instantly, she faced forward and gripped the wheel, seeing blinding headlights headed directly toward her. At eighty miles per hour, there was no chance of slowing down fast enough. She assumed the police were out to get her. Her heart thumped as she swerved to avoid the impact of the oncoming vehicle. In the blink of an eye, the sixteen-passenger van smashed head on into the Range Rover.

Glass splattered from all the windows as the front of the truck crumbled like paper. The police car that had been noticed by Carlie backed up after seeing the horrible crash. The officer rushed to the scene and called for an ambulance. Even though the response was rapid, and baby Kyla was rushed to the hospital, there was no chance to save Carlie. Her injured, gruesome-looking body hung out the car like a rag doll. Within minutes, it was clear - *dead on the scene.*

Also by Azarel

A life filled with fast money and violence lands twenty-three year old Candice Holmes in a witness protection program designed to keep witnesses safe. When Candice finds out that no one is capable of saving her from the wrath of the ruthless family she is scheduled to testify against, she finds herself on the run.

With nowhere to hide, she ends up fleeing to New York City where she is introduced to Daddy who owns a house where little girls are doing big things. Candice soon realizes that the street life she left behind is nothing compared to what goes on at Daddy's House. Between doing what it takes to survive and hiding her identity, Candice conquers one pitfall after another. Soon, all things come to an end when she goes toe-to-toe with the vicious woman who has the ability to put her six feet under, or sell her to the highest bidder.

Chloe is back and more conniving than before"
—Essence Magazine, Author of Deep

STILL A
Mistress
The Saga Continues

By *Tiphani*

Essence Magazine Best Selling Author
of The Millionaire Mistress

Lured by money and men, Still a Mistress explores the gritty
world of good girls gone bad. A year after the tragic death of
her family, Oshyn is still trying to piece together what's left of
her life. While struggling to return to a drama free world,
she is optimistic about her future. Little does she know that her
sister, Chloe, has reappeared to finish what she started, a
vindictive cycle of mayhem.

When Chloe finds herself in water that's too deep, a face from
her past comes back to haunt her. She ends up pulling out every
trick in the book, determined to make it to the top. Get ready to
enter a heart-pounding world of danger while Oshyn and Chloe
take you on a ride, you'll never forget. Still a Mistress is sexually
charged, and tests the boundaries of revenge when family vow to
fight until death.

Visit www.lifechangingbooks.net

Life Changing Books Titles

  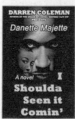 

 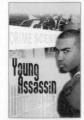  

ORDER FORM

MAIL TO:
PO Box 423
Brandywine, MD 20613
301-362-6508

FAX TO:
301-579-9913

Date	
Phone	
E-mail	

Ship to:	
Address:	
City & State:	Zip:
Attention:	

Make all checks and Money Orders payable to: **Life Changing Books**

Qty.	ISBN	Title	Release Date	Price
	0-9741394-0-8	A Life to Remember by Azarel	08/2003	$ 15.00
	0-9741394-1-6	Double Life by Tyrone Wallace	11/2004	$ 15.00
	0-9741394-5-9	Nothin' Personal by Tyrone Wallace	07/2006	$ 15.00
	0-9741394-2-4	Bruised by Azarel	07/2005	$ 15.00
	0-9741394-7-5	Bruised 2: The Ultimate Revenge by Azarel	10/2006	$ 15.00
	0-9741394-3-2	Secrets of a Housewife by J. Tremble	02/2006	$ 15.00
	0-9724003-5-4	I Shoulda Seen it Comin' by Danette Majette	01/2006	$ 15.00
	0-9741394-4-0	The Take Over by Tonya Ridley	04/2006	$ 15.00
	0-9741394-6-7	The Millionaire Mistress by Tiphani	11/2006	$ 15.00
	1-934230-99-5	More Secrets More Lies J. Tremble	02/2007	$ 15.00
	1-934230-98-7	Young Assassin by Mike G	03/2007	$ 15.00
	1-934230-95-2	A Private Affair by Mike Warren	05/2007	$ 15.00
	1-934230-94-4	All That Glitters by Ericka M. Williams	07/2007	$ 15.00
	0-9774575-2-4	The Streets Love No One by R.L.	05/2007	$ 15.00
	0-9774575-0-8	A Lovely Murder Down South by Paul Johnson	06/2006	$ 15.00
	0-9791068-2-8	Changing My Shoes by T.T. Bridgeman	05/2007	$ 15.00
	1-934230-93-6	Deep by Danette Majette	07/2007	$ 15.00
	1-934230-96-0	Flexin' & Sexin by K'wan, Anna J. & Others	06/2007	$ 15.00
	1-934230-92-8	Talk of the Town by Tonya Ridley	07/2007	$15.00
	1-934230-89-8	Still a Mistress: The Saga Continues by Tiphani	11/2007	$15.00
	1-934230-91-X	Daddy's House by Azarel	11/2007	$15.00
	1-934230-87-1-	The Reign of a Hustler by Nissa A. Showell	11/2007	$15.00
	0-9741394-9-1	Teenage Bluez	01/2006	$10.99
	0-9741394-8-3	Teenage Bluez II	12/2006	$10.99
			Total for Books:	$

Shipping Charges (add $4.00 for 1-4 books*) $

Total Enclosed (add lines) $

For credit card orders and orders for over 25 books
please contact us @ orders@lifechangingbooks.net
(cheaper rates for COD orders)

*Shipping and Handling on 5-20 books
is $5.95. For 11 or more books, contact
us for shipping rates. 240.691.4343